She knows what lonely men want most is a smile.

THE COLLECTED WORKS OF NOAH CICERO

VOLUME I

Lazy Fascist Press
an imprint of Eraserhead Press
205 NE Bryant Street
Portland, Oregon 97211

WWW.LAZYFASCISTPRESS.COM

ISBN: 978-1-62105-091-9

Edited by Cameron Pierce

Interior Design by Cameron Pierce and Kirsten Alene

Proofread by Sarah Baker

Printed in the USA.

Table of Contents

I Clean in Silence

When I take a shower, I like to wash myself at least four times with shampoo. I must get clean, I absolutely must get clean. Then I wash with special face wash that costs sixteen dollars but I got it half off because my mother is an Avon lady. Tom bitches if I spend too much on face wash; he's real obsessed with how much money I spend. I don't know why, it's my money. I work hard for my money and if I decide not to save because I want things right now, well, he can just fuck himself. I like things; I need things; things are what get me through the day. Without things, what is a woman? She's a man.

I've just finished taking my shower. It was a beautiful shower. I got to wash myself a complete four times. I feel so very clean. I'm a clean girl. I feel secure when things are decontaminated. That the world isn't so dirty, that I'm not so dirty. It's human to want to be washed. You know, we aren't living in the jungle anymore. Things need to be clean.

Things need to be cleaned because there is bacteria everywhere. Bacteria in the sink, bacteria in the shower, bacteria on the couch, *bacteria everywhere*. I can't stand bacteria. I consider it my job to kill bacteria, to vanquish all bacteria from the world. See, bacteria causes you to get sick, and I don't have health insurance so I can't get sick. Tom says if I get sick I should just die because I can't afford to pay back the bills. Maybe he's right, death can't be that bad. People have been doing it for millions of years. Another good thing about death is that I wouldn't have to deal with bacteria anymore. I wouldn't have to deal with family anymore, my insane father who sits on a stool in the kitchen farting and reading books about Hitler all day. Also my sisters. One's name is Cindy. She just tried to kill herself because her boyfriend broke up with her. She had to get her stomach pumped but she never even went to the mental ward. She just went home, sat down on the couch with a bottle of vodka and cried. My other sister, Julie, steals everything I own, like toothpaste, face wash, soap, and my vibrator. She stole my vibrator, can you believe that? My vibrator. What a sick bitch. Then she returned it three days later. Probably unwashed.

After Tom and I use the vibrator we always use anti-bacterial soap. Because we don't want to catch any diseases. I won't even let him buttfuck me without a condom.

I feel sick here standing in front of the mirror. My stomach hurts so much, so does my back, my breasts are too big and it causes my back to hurt. My skin hurts too. I don't know why so much of me hurts. I wish Jesus would take my pain away. I really wish he would. Oh, my stomach hurts. It hurts so much.

Nobody believes me when I'm in pain. Everyone accuses me of faking. I don't know why they accuse me of faking. Don't they know somebody in pain can go to work and be laughing and smiling and still be very sick? I'm so sick, I want to go to the doctor. But I can't because I have no health insurance. Well, it only costs fifty dollars to go to the doctor, but I can't afford pills. And I need so many pills, I'm in such great pain.

Now that I'm done with my shower I have to start arranging my hair. It takes a long time. I have to put four different kinds of product in it. One to make it firm, one to make it curly, another to make it shiny, and another to make it bouncy. I need all of them. I have to look perfect; people might see me. Even though I'm not leaving the house today, well I might go to Denny's, but a girl's gotta look good. That's another thing that separates men from women is that women gotta look good. Especially in Trumbull County. A girl has to look good, or her man will stop loving her.

Another thing is that I have to look good for Tom. It's important that I look beautiful for him constantly. Because he might leave. I'm sure he'll leave me, I just don't know when. See, he's in college and a real intellectual type. He reads a lot and talks to other kids who read a lot and I never understand what they're talking about. I don't admit that I don't know what they're talking about. Instead I just call him arrogant. I know it's wrong, but I do. That's who I am, and I can't change for anything. I would like to be intellectual like him, but I can't focus when I read. And I definitely can't go to college. I could never walk on a campus. All those people I've never met surrounding me. I would get lost and never find my class. I would flunk out; I would have to talk to my father.

The real worry is that Tom will leave me for an intellectual girl. I know he will. I know he will. One day some girl in one of his classes with a real nice ass and a perfectly thin stomach who knows a lot of big words will steal him away from me. I know it'll happen. I know I'll never be good enough for him.

Next thing I have to do is fix my face. First I have to put cream all over it to cover up my blemishes. I have a huge pimple right next to my nose. There's so much white juice in it. It's disgusting. I must pop it. I must. I get real close to the mirror and pinch with my two fingers. The white cream won't come out. Maybe I should leave it alone. No, it must come out. I will not have a pimple full of white shit on my face. I pinch and pinch. Finally the white juice comes and so does blood. It won't stop bleeding. I immediately grab some toilet paper and rip off a little shred and place it on the pimple. I want to cry. Now it'll look horrible. How can I go outside looking this horrible? Tom will not love me today. He'll hate me and leave me.

To cover up the bloody zit I glop a ton of cream on it. It's not helping, I'm fucked. I just go on and do my eyes. Then I curl my eyelashes. I know no one can tell when a girl curls her eyelashes, but I do them anyway. I have to; I can't go outside looking like a dirty white trash whore. I must look pretty.

I go into the bedroom and in there is a tall mirror. I take off my towel and stare at myself. I'm so fat, I'm so grotesquely fat. My legs are too short and chubby. My stomach protrudes; my arms are only one foot long. And my cunt, it's too big. How can Tom love me, I'm so disgusting. I hate looking at myself. Especially because I know Tom loves thin girls. I see him look at models in magazines and on television. He sees those thin bodies and wants them. He doesn't want mine. I'm so gross. God, I hate my mother for giving me this body. It's so boyish. Tom told me, he said my body is boyish. Why does he love my body?

I have to cover this gross body up so I can disguise the shittiness of it. I put on a small yellow shirt that shows my cleavage. Then tight blue jeans and little dark blue socks. I look good, I think.

Now I have to clean the house. I've been waiting to for the last two days. See, I live with Tom, my father, my two sisters, and our dear and lovely friend Sidney. Sidney cleans sometimes. I think he cleans better than me, but I won't admit it. I won't admit that someone, especially a man, cleans better than me. I have to do something good, don't I? God, I hope I do something good. I can't even get praised when I play video games. Sidney does better than me and Tom praises him because he has finesse. Well, why can't he praise me? I'm good too. I want to be good at something.

No one in my house is good at anything. We're not allowed to be. My father won't let us. He doesn't want anyone to be as great and perfect as he is, so every time we get close to achieving greatness and beauty, he tells us that we suck and asks what's wrong with us. I wish I could love my father. My father is a man, and so is Tom.

Tom wants me to do beautiful things, but I don't believe him. How can I? He's a man. Men don't want women to do good things. Men want women to clean the kitchen and change diapers.

I go out to the living room and look around. There are dirty plates on the coffee table, cups with soda left in them on the floor, beer bottles on the end table, my socks, shirts, and pants scattered throughout the room. All the clothes left in the living room are mine, I wonder why that is.

Now it's time to clean. I think about turning on the radio but I decide not to. I don't even turn on the television. There's no point in it. I want silence. I want to think. I need to think. I can't stop thinking. I also must keep moving. I can't stop moving or at least be watching a good show. I can't stand being inert. When I'm not distracted, I start thinking. Remembering too. I hate memories. I have so many. If I stop for one moment, I remember moments from when I was a child. Such bad moments, so much humiliation, so much mortification. If I stop moving I'll die, the world and its ugliness will consume me. I don't want to know or understand the world. Tom tells me about the world. How there are wars, starving mothers, crying children, suicide bombers, genocide, disease, the ozone disappearing. Oh, I hate it so much. I hate it when he talks about it. He does it so objectively too, like he doesn't care, like he supports it. I hate it so much. That's why I keep moving, because if I don't I'll be reminded of the world. Then I'll start crying. I'll lie on the floor in the fetal position, start pulling out my hair, and just pant and cry. I cry because I'm powerless. I have no power and it hurts. Hell, I don't even think I'm respected.

Every day I make up a new dream but I just give it up by the end of the day because I know there's no point in it. I'll die soon, I know it. If I don't die in a car wreck or of natural causes, I guess I'll just have to kill myself. Maybe Jesus will come back and save us. He'll take all the sinners to hell and all the good people to heaven. Luckily, I'm a good person.

My first stage of cleaning is to gather up all the dishes and put them in the sink. I go around the room grabbing them up. Finally, I have them all in the sink. Then I turn the hot water on and pour some soap in it. I put a lot of soap in it because it's very important to get the dishes clean. There's a lot of bacteria on dishes, a lot.

I'm so sad. I can't restrain myself. I cry as I wash the dishes. The future is coming. I know it is. I have no money, I have no health insurance. I can't save, I want things. I can't be loved. I can't be myself. I work so hard and all they give me is money.

I want the beauty of the west, the mountains, rocky coasts, sea urchins, long strips of highway, endless fields and clear rivers. But all I have are these dishes. Dirty dishes that must be cleaned. Everything must be cleaned.

The Human War

Two hours till war.

It's six o'clock. Bush said at eight, people must die.

I'm going to Kendra's.

I'll hide out there. Are the terrorists coming?

I'm standing in my living room at my parents' house. My dad is sitting on his special seat, my mom on the couch, and my brother on the reclining chair.

They're watching the news.

The news isn't saying much.

My brother says he's going to fight on the side of Iraq.

My dad tells him to watch what he says. My brother doesn't care. He rambles on about money and oil.

My mother sits there quiet.

My dad doesn't know what to make of it. He's confused, but it's entertaining, and that's why he's watching.

War is entertaining.

I can't take their insanity anymore, so I leave.

Each minute, the war gets closer.

I grab my keys, and put on my beret.

I leave.

I head out to my car. Turn it on and drive away.

A guy is on the radio talking about the war.

Speculating.

Speculating.

Speculating.

He says in less than two hours, we shall fight to preserve freedom.

Freedom.

America wants to give another country freedom. That doesn't sound that bad, or does it.

I hope the terrorists don't attack. I read in the paper a couple of days ago that the terrorists would fuck up America if we attacked Iraq. I hope they were just trying to scare us.

They probably won't attack Youngstown, Ohio. There is nothing here of any importance. It will probably be New York again.

I went to New York City and nobody spoke English there. I felt as if I wasn't even in America. Like I was on some strange island full of all the nationalities of the earth. Not America.

But what is America.

I've seen a lot of America. Oregon, California, New York City, Nebraska, Arizona, Florida, South Carolina, and the New England area. In all those places I found completely different people. People who had no relation to each other.

They all lived under freedom though.

None of them cared though.

They just wanted their home and their family to be safe.

That's all.

The guy talks on the radio about war.

I listen and don't know whether to care or not.

Should I care, or not care. That is the question.

I'm on a lot of medication. It's hard to care; I'm numb all the time.

Every day has the same weather when you're on medication.

The sun is neither out nor hid away by clouds. It just doesn't matter.

I feel weird.

There is a lot of darkness this evening.

War.

I remember when I was little, watching the Gulf War on television. I wasn't scared, I was excited by it.

Now I'm scared.

I get to Kendra's.

I knock on the door of the trailer. Kendra opens the door.

There she is.

Kendra and all the history we've had together.

Kendra and I have known each other since we were fifteen. We are now both twenty-two. We've dated off and on since then. We have said I love you to each other many times over the course of seven years.

We were engaged last year for ten months. Then I had a threesome and told her.

I told her because I wanted to hurt her.

We go into the living room. She sits down on the couch, and I sit on the floor.

"What's up?" Kendra says.

"I've been walking the world alone."

"I walk the world alone too, but I like it that way."

"Why, doesn't it get to you?" I say.

"No, it doesn't. I can do my own thing all the time. No one is bothering me; no one is fucking with my shit. Who needs people, when you have yourself."

"You remain because you don't like people judging you."

"I know, I hate to have people thinking about me. I always think they're thinking bad about me," Kendra says.

"People think you're great."

"Yeah, but I don't believe them."

We sit in silence for a second.

"Turn on the war," I say.

"Fuck no, I don't care."

"You don't care?"

"Why should I care? It doesn't have anything to do with me."

"Because it's interesting."

"It's not interesting, it's fucked up. I don't have any time for war. I have things to do."

"Like what?" I say.

"Paint my bathroom, and make curtains."

"You're right, you don't have time for the war."

"War is absurd. Human beings shooting at each other. That doesn't make any sense," Kendra says.

"Nothing makes sense. I thought America was civilized."

"We're not, honey," Kendra says.

"I don't wanna live in an uncivilized nation."

"You have to, for me, I need you."

"You need me. Why? I don't do anything for you, and I piss you off most of the time."

"Because you're the only person I can really talk to."

"I talk pretty well to you too," I say.

"You believe in the war, don't you?"

"No, don't accuse me of that."

"No, you're lying, you love Bush."

"I fucking hate Bush. You're insane."

"You want people to die, don't you?" Kendra says.

"No, leave me alone."

"You want world domination. I know you do."

"I don't know what I want, but I don't want that."

"You're cute," Kendra says politely.

"Thanks."

"Last night I cried."

"Why?"

"The terrorists are coming to get me. They're going to put smallpox in the air, I know it. We'll all be dead in a week, and Jesus will come back," Kendra says.

"Jesus won't come back, and you won't die in a week."

"Jesus will come back and send Bush to hell for everyone to see."

"That would be nice," I say.

"Jesus doesn't like wars. He said to walk the extra mile."

"Bush doesn't care about that verse."

"He should, he says he's Christian."

"He's Christian for votes," I say.

"I'm going to kill him."

"You are?"

"Yes."

"How?"

"I'm going to shoot a missile at the White House while he's sleeping in there all snug in his bed," Kendra says.

"Where are you going to get a missile."

"I'll find one. It can't be that hard."

"You should do it then, for your mental health."

"Yeah, it would release a lot of pent-up aggression," Kendra says.

"What are you going to do after you kill the president?"

"I'm going out to get drunk and celebrate."

"Good idea."

"Then I'll go to college to become a doctor."

"I thought you hated college."

"I guess you're right. I guess I'll stick to being a pizza delivery girl," Kendra says.

"Yeah, you are really good at it. I don't see why you should stop now."

"I know, I am good at it," Kendra says.

"I don't want to be an American anymore," I say.

"Leave then."

"Where can I go? I have no money, and no passport."

"Go to Mexico."

"I went there already, I got robbed," I say.

"Go nowhere then."

"How will I get there."

"By train."

"That's too expensive."

"Drive your car."
"I have no insurance."
"Reject the absurd, and kill yourself," Kendra says.
"I'm afraid of death."
"Don't be afraid, Jesus saves."
"I don't believe in Jesus."
"No one does."
"Can America save me?"
"Only you can save yourself."
"I have no interest in being saved," I say.
"That might be the cause of your problems."
"I don't have problems."
"You have only yourself."
"I don't want myself," I say.
"No one does."
"There's a war."
"I don't care."
"No one does."
"What if America loses," Kendra says.
"Then the troops go home, and some don't."
"Then mommies cry."
"A lot more Iraqi mothers will cry."
"Yeah, but they don't matter."
"Why don't they matter?" I say.
"They aren't Americans, they're evil."
"What if they aren't evil?"
"If they aren't evil, why are we killing them?"
"Money."
"Someone will lose their existence for money?"
"Yes."
"I would never give up my existence for money," Kendra says.
"I wouldn't lose my existence for anything, except freedom."
"We already have freedom."
"Then we don't need to lose our existence."
"As a child, I never thought of war."
"War is for old people with money," I say.
"War is fought by young boys who don't have very high IQs."
"They choose to fight."
"Then we can't blame them," Kendra says.
"Who can we blame?"

"No one, I guess."

"I'm tired of this," Kendra says.

"What?"

"America and its civilization."

"A lot of people are weary of it."

"I'm tired."

"But no one is listening."

"I am the voice crying in the wilderness," Kendra says.

"But no one hears."

"You hear, don't you?"

"No."

"When I'm alone, I cry."

"And still no one hears."

"I want my tears to be seen by America, I want my tears on public television."

"America doesn't want your tears," I say.

"What does it want?"

"Blood."

"I have only tears to give."

"America wants war, it wants humans dead."

"I'm human."

"They want you dead," I say.

"Why would a human want to kill another human?"

"Power, silly."

"Power?"

"Yes, power."

"I have no power."

"No one does."

"I don't know what I would do if I had power."

"You'd misuse it," I say.

"I probably would."

"Everybody does."

"Is there no way we can stop this war?"

"It's impossible."

"Existence is impossible."

"Existence is war."

"I don't want to fight anymore."

"You have to fight."

"I don't want to," Kendra says.

"No one does."

I look at Kendra's face, it is beautiful.

There is pain in it.

She is beat down by this world.

I forgive her for being mad.

When I first met her, she was innocent. Now she's scarred and putrid. She is in a constant struggle for survival. But she goes on, she fights even though she doesn't want to.

I love to listen to her talk.

I'm heartbroken.

The bombs will soon drop.

Bush will be happy.

Kendra lays there, smoking. I stare at her. I love her for a moment. She is so worried.

I reach out my hand and pet Kendra's face.

She purrs like a kitten.

I imagine people dying. I see parents crying, and little children without legs.

I don't want to be an American any longer.

I want to be in Mexico drinking cerveza in a whorehouse. I want to smoke some meth and forget I ever existed.

I am never going to forgive America for this.

I thought this was a democracy.

Plato didn't believe in democracy.

Little children will watch this on television and wonder. They will get no real answers though; no one cares about real answers.

I thought the world was changing for the better.

People change when they grow up.

They change for the worse.

They start worrying about money. Money becomes an all-consuming thought. Then they die.

I have no interest in dying.

But I have to. I have to care one day about things that don't matter to me.

I look at Kendra and think, I used to love her. But I don't anymore. But I tell her 'I love you,' I tell her so many things.

She's monogamous to me, but I'm not to her. Though I still feel like I'm taking care of her. She knows I date other people, but she puts up with it. She's so weak and fragile. I don't know what keeps her alive.

There is so much pain.

Absurdity.

Kendra crawls next to me. She wraps her body around mine. I hold her tight to me. Then I kiss her on the eyelids.

"I love you," she says.

"I love you too," I say.

I don't know why I say that. I don't mean it.

I say it because I have to.

I say a lot of things because I have to.

I live a useless existence.

Do I love Kendra? Most likely no. I love no one. I walk the world alone.

I'm not fit for human consumption.

I used to be able to love. But I can't anymore. It's too hard. And I especially can't love while a war is on.

I want to love Kendra, but it's destroyed now since I've cheated.

And I like promiscuous sex too much.

It would be nice to hold the same person on a regular basis, but it gets boring. I grow weary of their bodies.

I'm a hard man to please.

I don't stay pleased for long.

Who am I, I ask myself.

Perhaps I'll never know.

I never know why I'm incapable of love.

Love is for mediocre people.

Intelligent people can't love.

We know too much about the madness.

Love is madness.

All human interaction is madness.

I never wanted to be a human.

This is not my fault.

The war is not my fault.

Every day I look at myself.

And I amaze myself.

At the things I do because of jealousy, the pursuit of power, and insecurity.

I don't recognize myself.

But there I am.

A monster.

An animal.

A monkey.

A human.

An American.

I never asked to be any of those things, I'd much rather be a dolphin or a butterfly. It would even be better to have been a cat.

I've punched so many time clocks.
And I've never been paid enough.
And I've never worked hard enough.
I'm not very responsible.
I don't really care about anything.
I never could find a reason.
Or maybe I don't have the energy.
There better be a God. Someone needs to answer for this.
I need answers.
I need to understand my suffering.
And my happiness.
Why the world is absurd.
I've read a million books. And I don't think it has made my life better.
Maybe worse.
I cry.
The last winter was cold. It snowed almost every day.
I almost killed myself last winter.
I quit my job, and ran away to New York City in December. I spent five hundred dollars in three days on strippers, beer, and poetry.
When I got home, I had no money. I had to buy Christmas presents with my parents' money.
I almost killed myself.
Please pity me.
It feels good to be pitied.
Absurdity.
I cried so many times in the winter.
But it didn't solve anything.
All my problems were still there.
They weren't big problems. But they were big to me.
I hate when people belittle each other's problems. Problems are proportionate to the person's brain they involve.
Someday I'll walk free again.
I'll walk in the desert of Arizona, smiling, with a bottle of cold water.
I'll laugh at these days.
Too bad that the people who will die in this war will still be dead.
I'll be alive.
And I'll go on for them.
I'll walk to the bottom of the Grand Canyon. I'll stand there like I'm in heaven. I'll be strong and powerful standing there with my feet in the Colorado River.

But they'll still be dead.
I have to go on.
I have to fight the good fight.
Absurdity.
Civilization was started in Mesopotamia.
Which is in Iraq.
This is where civilization has led us.
To technological war.
People will die.
I've never met them.
But I'm sure.
They had hopes.
Moms.
Dads.
Brothers.
Sisters.
They had people who loved them.
But they must die.
Because they follow orders from an asshole.
An asshole is a person who orders other people to kill other people.
Bush could be an asshole.
In the Old Testament, God said, "Eye for an eye."
Jesus said turn the other cheek.
But Jesus no longer matters.
Especially to people who say they believe in Him.
Christian Republicans love war.
They love money too.
They hate homosexuals.
And young girls who get abortions because they have no money to raise their children.
I don't know God.
I don't know what He wants.
They say He left a book explaining His likes and dislikes.
But it's too full of contradictions, and it lacks historical proof.
For me to take it seriously.
I grew up in the information age.
Science is my god.
I was taught only science could save me from the horrors of this world.
Not some mystical god.
I believe that there are ghosts.

But I don't know what that means.
I don't believe there are absolute truths.
Perhaps I don't even care about truth.
It's not like knowing the truth changes anything.
Money changes things.
And I don't have any money.
So I can't change anything.
I've been broke for three months now.
My parents give me five dollars a day to buy cigarettes and get coffee.
But I just got my income tax check back.
I got two hundred and seventy dollars.
Tonight I'm going to spend some.
That's my plan.
I'll escape from this war with money.
Money can save me from suffering.
My mother makes sixty thousand a year.
She still bitches about money.
If you gave her a million dollars, it still wouldn't be enough.
Nothing is enough for her.
And most other people.
I watch the people of the world.
They're dissatisfied.
Nothing is enough for them.
They have no peace.
They are constantly disgruntled.
I want to pet their faces and tell them it will be all right.
But I know it will not help.
Existence.
No matter where you are.
It's hard.
Humans are an unhappy animal.
They live long lives with memories.
Jobs.
Religions.
Choices.
Families.
And never any answers.
Humans seek answers constantly.
But they know there are none.
The universe is answerless.

People are victims of their psychologies.

They can never escape the truth that their mind has made for them.

The people of the world are shattering under the immense power of civilization.

Absurdity.

"Kendra, touch my penis," I say to her calmly.

She reaches her little hand in my boxers and fondles my penis.

"Touch my cunt," Kendra says politely.

I reach my big hand in her underwear. I begin rubbing her clitoris.

We both make noises.

I place my mouth to hers and kiss softly.

I put my other hand in the back of her pants and touch her buttocks.

She has a beautiful body.

I love touching her.

She is so soft.

I pull off her shirt.

Revealing her young firm breasts concealed within a bra.

I kiss the tops of her breasts.

Then her tummy.

Then I go back to kissing her lips.

She is still fondling my penis.

I'm still rubbing her clitoris.

Her vagina slowly becomes wet.

I plunge my fingers in.

She makes louder noises.

I love to hear a woman's soft voice make animal noises.

Her eyes close.

She takes off her bra.

I take off my shirt.

She lies on top of me.

Her naked chest is petal-like against my chest.

We kiss like maniacs.

Pulling hair.

Rolling around on the floor.

I put her nipple in my mouth.

And suck with tender care.

Her vagina becomes wetter.

She loves to have her nipples sucked.

I take off her pants.

I kiss her thighs.

And rub my hands up and down them.
I take off my pants.
The only clothes left on are our underwear.
I pull hers off.
She pulls mine off.
We stand before each other naked.
I jam my penis into her vagina.
We do it missionary.
Her eyes remain closed.
I'm in love with her for a moment.
I go back and forth.
Noises are made.
The world doesn't exist.
Suffering doesn't exist.
There are no problems during sex.
I tell her to get on top of me.
We disconnect and she gets on top.
She puts me back in.
She goes up and down.
"People are going to die in a little bit and we're fucking," I say.
"What else can we do?"
"I don't know, it just feels like there must be something we should be doing."
"All we can do is fuck."
"But we're having so much pleasure, and people are going to be suffering so intensely in just a little bit."
"Listen Mark, there's nothing we can do. This war doesn't have anything to do with us. We're peasants, we don't matter," Kendra says.
"But I'm human, and I'm affected by this war."
"You're not affected, you mean nothing, you are shit in the big picture. We are all shit."
"I'm tired of being shit," I say.
"Get used to it."
"Why did my parents bring me into this world."
"Because women have a baby fetish," Kendra says.
"Women only have babies because they want attention."
"People love attention."
"Sex is the ultimate act of getting attention."
"That's why I have it."
"I know," I say.

"You know me too well, I can't love you."

"It's funner to love someone who really doesn't know you."

"I know you like a brother," Kendra says.

"I know, it isn't fun like it used to be."

"It used to be so fun, but now, we sit around like we're brother and sister watching television. The only difference is that we have sex."

"You're so good at fucking, I can't resist," I say.

"You're good too."

"Thank you."

"I love fucking you."

"I love fucking you too, I feel like I love you when we fuck."

"Me too."

"We've been fucking for seven years. Will this ever stop?" I say.

"I know I can't go on with my life because I keep fucking you."

"Who cares about going on with one's life, this is all life is."

"Life isn't much."

"No it isn't," I say.

"Once upon a time we were children, Mark, we were little and we played games, and smiled. Now look at us, the only time we can smile is when we're fucking."

"It's a sad state we're in."

"I want more from life, I want to live my dreams."

"How come you can't?"

"I can't leave the house, and I don't have any dreams."

"Everyone dreams."

"I don't."

"You should," I say.

"What could I be, a fireman, a rock star, what could I possibly be?"

"A painter, a writer, something, you just have to do something, you have to get motivated."

"I'm tired of trying to be motivated. Too much has happened to me to ever get motivated again," Kendra says.

"What has happened?"

"Well, first when I was little girl someone decided to molest me repeatedly, then my father beat me constantly, and he never spoke to me. My Elektra complex is all fucked up," Kendra says.

"I know, a lot has happened to you... But you have to go on, you have to keep trying."

"I don't want to try anymore, I'm done trying. I work at Pizza Hut. That's my life now. Pizza."

"You have such a beautiful personality, you could be a star."

"I can't be anything. What for? It's not like it will really matter. Someday I'll die, and hopefully there's a heaven, and that's all I can hope for now."

"There's so much more, Kendra."

"There's only me and my madness."

"I worry about you, I worry that one day I'll come over and you'll be dead because you've killed yourself, or you'll be in the mental ward."

"I'm fine, I can operate in the real world. I can work, I can function."

"I know. You function well."

"I'm worried about you. You don't function at all," Kendra says.

"You're right, I don't."

"You don't go to work, you cry all the time, and you're constantly having panic attacks. You're trapped in this world of shit, and I don't know if you'll ever get out of it. You used to be so full of hope and vigor. Now you're like a lost man wandering alone in the desert."

"I am."

"Yes, you are, you're lost. You're so smart and powerful, but you're just wasting it. I don't have a chance, but you do. Don't waste it, Mark. Take advantage of your life. I know you could do anything if you just tried."

"I'm just in a slump right now, someday I'll get better."

"I know, you're just having a couple bad months."

"I'm going to take advantage of my life, I'm going to live it out to the end. When I die, people will admire and be jealous of my existence, and they will wonder how I did it all, how I lived such an exciting life."

"I know you have it in you."

"Someday we won't know each other, Kendra," I say sadly.

"I know, someday you'll move and never come back. You're not the kind of person to live in Ohio forever."

"It's not that I dislike Ohio, I just like other places better."

"Someday you'll be happy, Mark, someday life will mean something to you."

"But you, what about you. You need to try to live again, you need to make something of your life," I say.

"I have all I need, I have this trailer, and I make enough money to keep it. So what does it matter. I have everything I need."

"But you don't make enough money to go on vacation, or save up."

"I don't worry about that. My dad will give me money if I need it."

"I guess you're right about that."

During this whole conversation we remain having sex.

I flip her over.

Then I do her doggy style.

The war is on.

I look at her and think about how doomed she is.

How she is destroyed.

I shed a tear as I fuck her.

For her.

I pull out and have an orgasm onto her back.

I stare at it.

It is powerful lying there.

She turns around and kisses me on the lips.

Then she stands up and goes to the bathroom to wipe herself off.

I sit there happy.

The war will start soon.

This is my existence.

This is who I am, and what I do.

I don't know if I like it, or even care for it.

But I do it.

I go on having sex and drinking, not caring if I live or die.

I don't think I'm mentally healthy.

But I don't care anymore.

I've been suffering from depression since I was in ninth grade.

Since then I've been tormented.

Since then I've not wanted to be myself.

Kendra comes back into the room and lies next to me.

We light cigarettes.

There is love between us.

But I have cheated on her.

And she can never trust me again.

Therefore our love is destroyed.

I don't care.

I don't think she does either.

We are just two humans looking for an escape.

That's all.

We are alone.

And tired.

"I don't feel right," Kendra says.

"How do you feel?"

"I don't know... I don't feel human."

"I feel like that a lot of the time. Like I'm not part of the human race, I'm something else, something alone and mad," I say.

"I feel angry."

"You don't act it."

"But I am, I'm so angry. I'm so tired."

"Don't worry, life will get better."

"Perhaps," Kendra says.

Absurdity.

"You kiss other girls, don't you?" Kendra says.

"You're on a need to know basis, we aren't going out."

"I know you, and I can't help but feel jealousy."

"You went out on a date the other day and told me about it. What was that?"

"I told you, I thought about you the whole time."

"Don't think about me the whole time. Live your life. We don't love each other anymore, we can never be again," I say.

"But, I love you."

"You don't love me, you love the memories you have of me. All we do together is have sex. We give pleasure to each other's genitals, that's what we do, and that's all."

"But you mean so much more."

"I don't mean shit."

"I know, you don't. I don't even think about you when you aren't around."

"I don't think about you when you're not around either," I say.

We finish smoking our cigarettes, and then hold each other.

We lie there silent with our eyes closed.

I think about the night ahead of me.

I have to go to Denny's and read for a little bit. Then to the strip joint. Then to the bar for crapieoke.

I don't know what will happen tonight.

I hope something happens.

I stand up and put my clothes on.

She lies there quiet staring at the television.

"Where are you going tonight?" Kendra says.

"I'm going to Denny's to read, then to the bar for crapioke."

"You have fun."

"I will."

"Don't kiss any girls," Kendra says.

"I won't."

I kiss her on the lips and leave.

I get into my car.

The radio is talking about the war.

Useless speculation.

I don't know why I fucked Kendra.

I don't even know why I went over there.

I should just leave her alone.

But I can't.

There's something beautiful about her that I need.

Something my heart cries out for.

She could always make me laugh. Most women don't make me laugh.

I've known her for so long.

It's hard to live without her.

She is such a comfort to me in this time of crisis.

Since September Eleventh we've been in a crisis.

My father's generation had to fear the Communists.

Now we fear Arabs.

Most likely when the Arab problem disappears, America will find someone new to fear and fight with.

It's so childish to fight.

When I was in school, I fought a lot. They kicked me out of school.

People go to jail for killing people.

But a soldier becomes a hero.

I don't understand that.

I don't understand at all what America is doing.

And what Iraq is doing.

I don't understand at all.

I feel very alone.

I will walk this world alone, not understanding anything.

One hour till war.

I get to Denny's.

I go inside and see the glory of Denny's.

It's a shitty Denny's. It hasn't been refurnished for years. It's probably one of the worst Denny's in America.

I sit down at the counter.

I start reading Proust while I wait for someone to get me coffee.

A waitress named Cindy comes over.

She's about thirty.

She's white trash.

She's missing teeth.

"How are you doing today, Mark?"

"Good, how are you?"

"Oh, fine. Coffee?"

"Yeah."

She goes over and pours me a cup of coffee and puts it down in front of me.

I put two Sweet N' Lows in it. And stir.

Steam is coming up from the warm coffee.

I take a sip. It's still too hot to drink.

I go back to reading.

I love reading.

It's the only thing that keeps me together.

I need books.

I need those dead man's lines.

I need their truth.

I like writers that write out of necessity.

Writers who write because they have to.

Who are compelled to express.

They are driven by one thing only, and that is the written word.

I see books as the purest representations of an era.

When anthropologists a thousand years from now need to understand the psychology of the people of a time, they will look at their books. Not their bridges, computers, and skyscrapers.

There is an older black man sitting a couple of seats away from me at the counter. He suddenly says to me, "Civilization."

I look up from my book and reply, "Huh."

"Civilization."

"What about it?"

"I'm tired of it, that's why I moved into the woods."

"You moved into the woods?" I say.

"Yeah, deep in the woods of West Virginia."

"How's that?"

"It's beautiful. I live a peaceful life there, free from television, microwaves, computers, and religion. I'm free of everything technological and oppressive."

"Why don't you like civilization?"

"Civilization is war, a race, a battle for power. People are run by two things, jealousy and power," he says.

"You have a point there."

"People are primitive and too monkey-like. I can't stand them, and I can't stand myself either while I'm with them. They make me turn into an insane monster, that's what civilized people do to each other, they turn each other into monsters."

"I feel like a monster a lot."

"That's why I went to the mountains, I had to escape their madness. It's repulsive living in civilization... I didn't leave my cabin for a year, and then I decided to leave to go see my mother in Ohio. And I find out there's a war going on. It's disgusting!"

"You don't believe in the war?" I ask.

"No, I don't. I'm a pacifist. I believe all problems can be solved without violence. There is no need for violence. People react much better to peace."

"But war is part of being human. Violence is natural."

"Violence might be natural, but that doesn't mean we need it," he says.

"Perhaps we do need it."

"If we do need it, I'm glad I live in the woods."

"You're probably right. I wished I lived in the woods. Can I come with you back to West Virginia?"

"No, people are annoying."

"What happened to you to make you think this way about the world?"

"I was in Vietnam in the infantry. I killed a lot of people, a lot of innocent people."

"How many do you think you killed?"

"Over a hundred... I have to live my whole life knowing I took over a hundred lives away from people who deserved them just as much as I do."

"That sucks."

"No shit it sucks! I took orders to kill people, I could have said no, but I didn't, I said yes sir, and did it. I killed and while I did it I liked it. Then years later while I was driving my car I realized it, I realized that I killed people, that I took people's lives. Then I became depressed for several years. No one understood it; I was such a happy person... Then I became religious but that didn't help, so I bought a piece of land in West Virginia, and I've remained there ever since. Except for once a year I go and visit my mother."

"I can see why you're a pacifist."

"I have good reason to be."

"I think it's wrong how the government gets young stupid boys to join the military right after high school. Those kids are so dumb and naïve. It's like the government is taking advantage of them."

"I was once one of those young stupid boys. I was so dumb, I thought I was doing it for freedom; I wasn't doing anything for freedom. I fought for rich people that I would never meet. I should have become a hippy and protested. But instead I beat up hippies; I didn't know what the hell was going on. I was sure that what I was doing was right, but it was wrong, it was cruel and wrong."

"I'm sorry you have to live with that."

"Listen to me kid, never go into the military. Read your books, go to college, have sex, but never go into the military, they'll brainwash you, and make you believe that fighting for America has meaning. It doesn't. Personally I would only fight if a nation was directly attacking America. If they were bombing Yellowstone, or the Rocky Mountains, then I'd fight. But not for oil, fuck no!"

"You think this war all comes down to oil?"

"Listen, there are African and Latin American countries that have horrible tyrants just like Saddam and we aren't fighting them. So why should we pick on Iraq. I feel that unless we take care of all the countries that have tyrants, we shouldn't take care of any," he says.

"Yeah, but those countries don't have oil."

"You're right, they don't have anything we need... Well I have to go."

"See ya later."

He gets up and pays and then walks out.

I go back to reading.

I don't know what to make of what he said.

I guess an opinion on war would be most credible from someone who actually fought in a war.

I have no idea what war is.

All I know is that it doesn't sound fun.

I drink my coffee and smoke cigarettes.

Half an hour till war.

I feel like I should be sitting next to a television watching the speculations and reports, but I don't want to be home with my family listening to their speculations.

Everyone has an opinion, and I don't want to hear any of them.

Jimmy comes in and sits down next to me.

"Here again?" Jimmy says.

"Of course," I say.

"I sat in the park all day."

"How was that?"

"Peacefully full of turmoil."

"The war is going to start soon."

"Soon we will all be dead," Jimmy says.

"Are the terrorists coming."

"Why wouldn't they, if I were them I would."

"Maybe they'll bomb Denny's."

"They should, America revolves around this Denny's," I say.

"America hates Denny's."

"Of course they hate Denny's, Denny's is designed for poor people."

"And poor people are expendable."

"That's why they got mad about September Eleventh, because so many rich people died."

"And rich people shouldn't die."

"Should we become rich?" I say.

"Of course, it's the American dream."

"I'm the American dream."

"You surely are."

"I'm like Donald Trump."

"I know, you're a millionaire."

"I have millions, that's why I go to Denny's."

"Me too, I own oil wells in the Middle East," Jimmy says.

"I don't like this."

"Don't like what."

"This war."

"No one does."

"But we're saving a nation of people from a tyrant."

"But that's not our country," Jimmy says.

"So they should save themselves."

"Yes."

"But why shouldn't we save them?"

"I don't see why we wouldn't."

"Are you serious?"

"Yes."

"I thought you were against the war?" I say.

"I'm confused, I don't see why we should, and why we shouldn't."

"I'm confused too."

"We can be confused together."

"As we sit here and drink coffee."

"And smoke cigarettes."

"We can be confused," I say.

"Yes."

"I don't see any clear answers to any of my questions."

"One will never get clear answers when it involves the actions of the government," Jimmy says.

"The war is starting, it's eight o'clock."

"You're right, it is."

"Bombs have just been fired."

"Soon people will die," Jimmy says.

"And they will never get to live another day of life. They will never get to fuck again or get drunk with their friends."

"They have to die, so we can drive our cars."

"Maybe I would rather ride a bicycle than have people die."

"No you wouldn't, you'd rather have them die," Jimmy says.

"You're probably right."

"Who knows, maybe you would ride a bike."

"I can't bear this."

"It's bearable."

"I know, and that's what is painful," I say.

"There will be a lot of pain in upcoming weeks."

"I feel so powerless and frustrated."

"You are powerless."

"Each man must learn he is powerless one day."

"And a painful day that is," Jimmy says.

"I'm a human, I should be able to do something."

"There is nothing you can do, except be pissed."

"What if I light myself on fire like the Buddhists did in Vietnam?"

"You'll be on the news, but that's about all."

"The war will go on."

"The machine has started, now it won't end till it's over."

"The machine is unbreakable."

"The machine has been working strong for thousands of years, it won't end for you."

"What if I pray for a really long time?"

"Prayer doesn't help anyone, you know that."

"I feel so powerless, so small, so worthless," I say.

"You are powerless, small, and worthless."

"Tonight I'm going to get drunk and hopefully forget that I'm human."

"You should try that, it'll be good for you."

"I will, I'll get drunk."

"And what will you do then?"

"Go home and hang myself."

"Why would you do that?"

"Because I no longer want to live in a world where bastards wage war on each other."

"The bastards have to wage war, it's what they do... See, kids who want to be soldiers do it because they are warlike beasts; they have to fight to feel human."

"But civilians are getting killed."

"They will go to Allah," Jimmy says.

"What if there's no God?"

"Then they go nowhere."

"They disappear?"

"Yes."

"I don't want to die."

"Personally I don't think anyone does."

"Why do we do it then?" I say.

"Because we have to."

"I refuse."

"You don't have much choice."

"I should have a choice, I'm a free individual."

"We all die."

"What if there's no God?"

"Then nowhere."

"All my memories gone."

"Memories gone."

"But my memories make me who I am."

"Then you won't be anyone."

"I always want to be someone."

"Well, one day you won't be anyone."

"What will I do that day?"

"Nothing."

"Forever?"

"Yes, forever."

"There must be another option?"

"It's not even an option, it's an ultimatum," Jimmy says.

"I don't like imminent things."

"No one does."

"We should wage a war against death."

"We did, it's called religion."

"I thought religion was to make sure people hated homosexuals."

"No, it's a battle against death."

"Oh yes, if you believe in Jesus you will have everlasting life."

"See?"

"I see."

"So if you believe in Jesus, you shall have everlasting joy in heaven."

"What if Jesus was just a regular man like you and me?"

"Then it's not true," Jimmy says.

"Then for the last two thousand years people have been believing in a dumb guy who might have not even existed?"

"Possibly."

"Oh, this is maddening."

"Yes, it is."

"Could it be any worse?" I say.

"Probably not."

"Only if people knew that their lives were based off of bullshit, they don't know how bad the shit really is."

"No they don't, and they don't want to know, so don't tell them. They don't need to know."

"Will they ever figure it out?"

"Slowly they figure everything out."

"How long do we have to wait?" I say.

"Another thousand years if we don't blow each other up by then."

"I don't want to be blown up."

"It doesn't matter when you die, after you die the same thing will happen no matter when you die. Either heaven or nothing."

"I prefer heaven."

"We all do."

"Heaven sounds like a fairy tale though."

"I know, that's why it's absurd," Jimmy says.

"So all I am is a man on a rock, living a meaningless life, doing meaningless things, for meaningless reasons."

"Most likely."

"I don't want to be human anymore."

"No one does."

"But I've had experiences with ghosts, what does that mean?"

"Who knows?"

"You're right, who knows."

"Probably even the ghosts live a meaningless existence."

"It must be hard being a ghost. Sitting around all day in the same building, that must get boring and a little tedious."

"It has to be, I'd never want to be a ghost."

"When I die, there better be heaven, because I want an answer for this."

"Maybe heaven doesn't have an answer, and if they did, maybe you wouldn't accept it."

"If I'm in heaven, I have to accept everything."

"Why would you have to. There is always a chance for rebellion."

"And I prefer to be a rebel."

"It is always better to be a rebel. Following kills," Jimmy says.

"Following is for mongrels."

"There is no fun in following, but there is no fun in leading either."

"There is only fun in going alone, it is always better to be self-reliant."

"Self-reliance is the key to genius."

"Self-reliance is also the key to loneliness," I say.

"A long time from now we'll remember this day and not smile."

"No we won't."

Absurdity.

We sit in silence for several minutes.

The war has started.

I want a relationship, but it's hard.

Everyone that wants to go out with me is insane.

I can never find a sane girl.

Not that I want one.

I had one girl about a month ago.

She was in love with me too much.

She thought I was so smart and beautiful.

A lot more than I actually am.

I don't know what makes a certain person fall in love with another person.

My bet would be loneliness.

Most relationships I see, the two people in them don't have anything to do with each other. They just think each other are cute, so they begin a relationship.

I can't stand that.

But I guess there's more than that.

There's connection.

Like you have good conversation.

But I don't even see that in relationships.

I see a horny man and a woman who doesn't want to be alone.

There is so much sadness in this world.

Nobody wants to be alone.

So we thrust ourselves into relationships for reasons we don't even know.

But no one really knows the reasons why individuals do things.

Madness would be my guess.

I hang out with Kendra because we have good conversations together.
And she is really good in bed.
I don't know which one brings me back.
Most likely both equally.
I will always walk the earth loving Kendra.
I can't imagine loving anyone else but her.
I've loved her for so long.
Seven years.
We have so many memories together.
I would have to kill them all to go on.
And live a proper life.
I'm incapable of living a proper life.
Or showing real love again.
To anyone.
I used to say 'I love you' to Kendra with such sincere conviction.
But those days have passed.
Those days of happiness are over.
Now I'm left with the future and myself.
Absurdity.
"Jimmy, I spend all my money on sin," I say.
"Where else should it go?" Jimmy says.
"It seems like the poorer I am, the more I spend my money on vice."
"I thought you were broke. How do you have money to spend?"
"I got my income tax check."
"That's horrible to give to a broke person."
"Yeah, I know," I say.
"What did you spend it on?"
"Nothing yet, but I plan on going to the strip joint and getting drunk
at the bar. I figure it'll cost me like sixty dollars."
"Yeah, that sounds about right."
"But I know I shouldn't, I should save the money for better things."
"Who cares about saving money? You need sin. You're poor."
"I need sin to feel happy, to feel better about myself and this world."
"Sin is always good for that."
"You want to come with me to the strip joint?"
"Yeah, I'll go, I just got my income tax check too."
"Cool, then I don't have to sit there alone."
"Personally I love strippers. You can get touched by a woman without
having to ask her out, or take her out on a date."
"Yeah, that's why I go too."

"Don't tell anyone, but I like sin too."

"What sins do you like?"

"I like pills," Jimmy says.

"Uppers or downers?"

"Uppers, of course."

"How's that working for you?"

"Great, I have a three point eight in school."

"That does sound perfect."

"Damn straight."

"I like alcohol and strippers."

"When we were little children all we needed for happiness was to play hide and go seek, now we have to jam stimulates into us just to get through the day."

"I know, it's horrible," I say.

"But that's what it means to be human."

"To be addicted to things."

"Yes."

"I don't like being addicted to things, but I have to be, I must be."

"We are all compelled to madness."

"I hate being compelled, it's like I have no control over myself."

"What use is it to have control over yourself? That's so boring."

"And neither of us wants to be boring," I say.

"Being boring is premature death."

"My brother is boring, he's Christian Republican, he goes to work and plays golf, that's all."

"See, that's a horrible existence. I hope I always live an exciting life full of intellectual discovery," Jimmy says.

"I hope I don't die."

"You still worried about death."

"Of course I'm still worried about death."

"Don't be, it's not that big of a deal."

"I think it is."

"You think wrong, everything dies, it's the natural order of things."

"Once on television I watched an alligator kill a zebra. It seemed horrible, but it's the most natural thing there is."

"Maybe it's natural that we are killing people in Iraq."

"Maybe it is," I say.

"What is natural?"

"Anything that is biological."

"Is war biological."

"Aggression is biological, so I don't see why it isn't."

"War is natural then, so are we for or against the war?" Jimmy says.

"I suppose we're still against it," I say.

"Life is a war, this is just on a bigger scale."

"Perhaps."

"Maybe we should enlist."

"I don't think so."

"Why not, we could get to kill some Arabs."

"Well, when you put it like that."

"Yeah, it would be great, you and I out there in the desert getting shot at, shooting at people, killing them dead. Then staring at their dead bodies in the sand. Oh, it would be great."

"Yeah, that sounds so fun, killing people and looking at them dead lying in the sand."

"Oh, we would have a great time," Jimmy says.

"I think we should give an oil well to each of the families of the soldiers who die."

"Yeah, because those are the people who really deserve it, because they gave birth to a child who died for already rich people to get richer."

"And I also think after the regime is gone, they should make me president of Iraq."

"You would make a great president."

"I know I would."

"What is your platform for Iraq?"

"I would create the biggest military in the world and attack America."

"Good platform," Jimmy says.

"I believe I can crush them."

"So do I."

"Then I would take over the world, and pillage it of its resources."

"Another good idea."

"I would rage against anyone that said anything bad about me. I would paint the world red with blood."

"Man, you would make a great president."

"I know, it would be great. I think I'm going to call the White House tomorrow and ask them about it."

"You should, I bet they'll let you do it."

"Of course, who else would be qualified for the position."

"You, who else."

"Will you be my vice president?" I say.

"I'd rather be the head general of the army."

"Oh, even better. I won't have a vice president, who needs one."

"You certainly don't."

"I want to take over China and enslave them."

"That would be great, Americans would never have to do work again."

"There's enough of them to fill every occupation in America and Iraq. No one would have to work again."

"You're a political genius."

"I've studied a lot of Jefferson. That's where I get it from."

"I can see."

"If I took over America, I'd nuke West Virginia."

"Why?"

"It's a useless place, it doesn't need to be there anymore."

"Yeah, we don't need West Virginia," Jimmy says.

"Then I would put the White House in California."

"Good idea. Can I stay there in the Lincoln Bedroom?"

"Oh yeah, of course."

"Can I wipe my ass with a painting of Bush and Nixon?"

"No doubt, I wouldn't have it any other way."

"Beautiful."

"Do you want to go to the strip joint now?"

"Yes, that sounds perfect," Jimmy says.

We stand up and pay for our coffees.

The war has already started.

Planes are flying over Baghdad.

To throw bombs onto the city.

Buildings will soon be gone.

Toppled.

Screams will soon be heard.

Then they will go silent.

There will be mass death.

Americans will be glued to the television.

Parents of soldiers will sit at home worried.

Young infantry soldiers sit more worried.

There will be a lot of tears shed in the next few weeks.

I wonder if I will cry.

I hope not.

Death.

And then there was war.

I don't want this.

No.

I reject it.
I refuse to accept the world is like this.
But it is.
It's horrible.
And mad.
I do not know how to confront the day.
With this insanity.
I wish I were a child playing in the yard.
Or an old man sitting in a wheel chair.
But I'm not.
I'm young and I have to live with the memory of this for a long time.
How long will my life be.
Too long.
America has just begun to fight.
The clocks are burning.
Snakes are slithering through our hearts.
The animals are screaming in the wilderness.
There is no light here.
The prisoners are rioting.
The children are crying.
Christ is in heaven watching.
We all have scabies and we are scratching till we bleed.
Ulcers are hurting.
The sun is setting.
Lions stop hunting.
The moon is hidden behind the clouds.
There's a dust storm blinding us.
When I grow old.
This day will be a blur.
And it might not even matter.
Perhaps this is insignificant.
Perhaps the Iraqis will love freedom.
Perhaps they won't.
They never asked for freedom.
I don't see why we have to give it to them.
Of course I don't see why we don't.
But all the middle eastern countries are ruled by regimes.
Why save this one.
There are a lot of good questions that will never be answered.
Like we would believe the answers if they were told to us.

Someday I'll wake up and this will be over.
Until then I'll suffer.
I don't know why I suffer, I guess it's habit.
I no longer believe that there are solutions to the world's problems.
The world is controlled by humans.
And humans are an insane species.
They suffer from power.
I regret ever belonging to the human species.
It's trite and violent.
I would kill myself.
But I want to watch the insanity.
What will these crazy monkeys do next.
The human species is a train wreck.
They're all mangled and distorted.
They're all suffering from disorder of the mind.
And they're not very intelligent.
They have no desire to know anything.
And the ones who want to know.
Are so consumed with vanity they learn nothing.
I regret ever being an intellectual.
I'd rather be a mechanic.
Or something simple.
But I'm myself, and I know more than the next person.
I didn't choose this way of life.
It just happened that way.
By divine power or accident.
I don't know.
I don't believe in a way of life.
I don't think humans can follow any code of rules without fucking it up.
The Christian way.
The Taoist way.
The Buddhist way.
I don't believe in ways.
Humans are apes.
And apes can't follow ways.
They follow their instincts.
I used to believe in God.
And tried to live the Christian way.
But instead I followed my instincts.
Man is constantly at war with his instincts.

Man is constantly at war.
I used to believe in God.
But it faded.
As everything fades.
The saddest thing about existence.
Is that everything fades into the past.
The past is so remarkable.
In my past.
I failed kindergarten because I couldn't read.
I got into fights with schoolmates.
I scored touchdowns playing football.
I smoked weed.
Played in a band.
Had braces.
Got a root canal.
Had sex with a fat girl in a church.
Went to the mental ward.
Graduated from high school.
Lived in California and Oregon.
Went to Mexico and smoked meth.
All that lies in my past.
I was there for that.
That was me doing those things.
Now they're gone.
All part of the history of my existence.
And someday this will be part of my history on this planet.
There is much history in every person.
It's unbearable to think about.
We all live long lives.
Absurdity.
Jimmy and I get into our own cars.
The radio is announcing the beginning of the war.
We have already launched cruise missiles.
They are currently pelting Baghdad.
While I drive to the strip joint.
People are dying.
Buildings are being blown up.
Humans are scared.
Americans soldiers are celebrating because they hit their targets.
While I drive to the strip joint.

I'm happy.

There's no better place to take away a man's anguish.

I go to the strip joint every time I feel sad.

Even if I don't have money.

I go and get a lap dance.

I get some young girl to rub her butt on my penis.

It makes me feel better about being human.

Some say it's immoral that I go to strip joints.

But I don't care.

Everyone needs a little immorality in their life.

The war has started.

I get to the strip joint and walk in.

It's a little shitty place.

There's a small bar.

Only two men are there.

One old white guy wearing a button-down t-shirt.

He looks like he's retired from Packard and has money to spend.

The other one is an old black guy.

He looks like he still works but has money to spend.

Jimmy and I sit down at the bar.

There're two girls circulating the bar.

One is a mixed girl named China.

She's a beautiful girl.

I think she does coke.

And there's an ugly white girl.

I think she's an alcoholic.

I don't know why anyone would let that ugly white girl dance for them.

She's fucking putrid.

The girls' dressing room door is open. I see a pretty white girl getting ready in there.

It looks like Jamie.

Could it be Jamie?

I used to love Jamie this time last year.

I was obsessed with her.

I even wrote a book with her as the star.

She smells so good.

But she hasn't worked here in a while.

I was hoping she would be here.

She will take away all my suffering.

The girl walks out of the bathroom.

And it's not Jamie.

I wanted Jamie.

Jamie is so beautiful.

It's unreal.

I sit sad.

Absurdity.

"Jimmy, I feel like crying," I say.

"Why? You're at a strip joint, you should be happy."

"Because Jamie isn't here, I wanted Jamie. Where's Jamie? I want to find her."

"Dude, why do you care about Jamie? She's a whore."

"Because she was interesting, she was crazy. I love crazy girls."

"You need to stop dating crazy girls. All crazy girls do is fuck up your life."

"I don't care about my life, I want crazy girls," I say.

"You're sick."

"I'm not sick, I'm the pinnacle of normalcy."

"No, you're sick and mad."

"You could be right."

"None of these girls are very attractive," Jimmy says.

"This is the shittiest strip joint in America. What do you expect?"

"I don't know, attractive girls."

"All the attractive girls work at the Babylon, you know that," I say.

"I know, but that place is expensive."

"If you want hot girls, you got to pay the cash. Supply and demand, you know."

"Yeah, who cares? China is still hot though."

"You know it."

I watch China dance for the old white guy.

The old white guy loves it.

He smiles.

He knows there's a war.

We all do.

But the girls have to make money.

And the men have to get boners.

That is the law of the strip joint.

I always wanted to date a stripper.

But the girls never go out with me.

But fuck it, who cares.

So I've never dated a stripper.

And I probably never will.

That's existence.

Jimmy is sitting next to me, staring at the girl who's not Jamie swinging on the bar.

I look at the girl and don't care.

I want Jamie.

The girl is overweight anyway.

And she's really tall.

Which I despise in women.

I can't stand a woman to be above five foot five.

And she's like five nine.

Jimmy is enthralled.

He probably has a boner.

I don't have a boner.

I want one, though.

And I'm not leaving until I get one.

I got money and I want to spend it.

On perversion.

The song ends and the Jamie wannabe gets off the poll and comes over to me.

I stare at her as she walks over.

She stands before me: a tall red-headed giant.

"Hi, my name's Star. What's your name?"

I don't want to give her my name, she's not Jamie.

"Mark."

"Would you like a dance?"

I think about it for a long second.

I really don't want this girl to dance for me.

I'm not even attracted to her.

Kendra is better looking than her.

When you go to the strip joint, you're supposed to see girls hotter than the people you fuck.

"Yeah, I'll take a dance."

The song starts.

She begins bouncing her butt off my penis.

I'm not enjoying it.

I stare at China from across the room.

She's still trying to get money out of the old guy.

The redhead turns around and shows me her breasts.

Her nipples are pierced, of course.

She rubs her breasts in my face.

That is nice.

She does a bunch of other tricks to get me horny and get money out of me.

But they don't work.

I remain bored during the whole thing.

The song ends.

I give her a five.

She sits down next to me.

"So what do you do?" she says.

"I write," I say.

"What do you write about?"

"About what it means to be human."

"What does it mean to be human?" she says.

"I don't know."

"How do you write about it then?"

"I just write it."

"You just write it, that's it."

"Yes, I type, then it's all right there."

"Right there."

"Yes, right there."

"That's unbelievable."

"Yes, it can be at times."

"Do you have a real job?" she says.

"No, I'm unemployed."

"That sucks."

"What do you do in your spare time?"

"Raise my kids."

"Is that fun?" I say.

"No, it sucks."

"How old are they?"

"Not old enough."

"Do you beat your kids?"

"All the time."

"That's horrible for them."

"They don't care, they go right back to playing after I do it."

"Oh."

"Do you do coke?" she says.

"No."

"That sucks."

"Why?"

"Because I really want some."

"What kind of mother are you?"

"A bad one."

"I had a bad mother, kids never get over that shit," I say.

"I don't care, I'm not them," she says.

"You're right, you aren't them."

"I'm me, and I'm a stripper. I'm twenty-six years old. I've been a stripper since I was eighteen. I've done nothing with my life except get pregnant. You think I want to be me?"

"I wouldn't want to be you."

"I've never done anything all my life, I don't paint, write, anything creative. I've never tried to be anything. I've never wanted to be anything but drunk. I'm doomed."

"It must be tough to be doomed."

"It ain't easy."

There are a lot of doomed people.

They can't escape themselves.

I'm not the one to save them.

It's each person versus the universe.

Most lose badly.

I stare at her pretty face.

And wish there was some way I could save it from the madness.

But I can't.

I can only save myself.

I'm not Jesus.

So I just let her be.

She gets up and goes over to Jimmy.

She dances for Jimmy.

Jimmy is very happy.

He loves redheads.

I sit there in my sadness.

The ugly girl comes over and asks me for a dance.

I say no.

She walks away.

I order another beer.

I drink it fast, trying to get drunk.

China goes over and dances for the other old guy.

He puts his hands on her ass and rubs her bare butt cheeks.

I'm jealous.
I think about fucking China for a little bit.
Jimmy is still getting dances from the redhead.
I sit alone.
There's a war.
And I'm sitting in a strip joint.
I'm impatiently waiting for China.
All I want is a dance.
Then I can go to the bar and have a good time.
China finally comes over.
"Would you like a dance?" she says.
"Yes," I say.
She begins her dance.
I love her body touching mine.
I caress her butt the whole time.
My boner slowly rises.
She does the motions robotically.
I don't care, I want a boner.
She jabs her butt into my penis repeatedly.
My penis is at full length.
I love every second of it.
The song ends.
I ask her for another one.
She repeats the process.
My hard-on remains.
While she dances for me.
I forget everything.
All my suffering is gone.
I have a total moment of peace.
Tranquility.
Serenity.
Harmony.
The dance is over and I'm left blue-balled.
I give her ten dollars and she goes on her way.
I look over at Jimmy.
"I love being human," I say.
"Yeah, it's great."
"Let's get drunk."
"Okay."
We get the bartender to bring over shots.

We suck them down.

We sit smiling at each other.

We don't care about a damn thing in the world.

We order more beers.

"Remember September Eleventh?" I say.

"Yeah."

"I woke up and saw the towers destroyed on television."

"That's quite a thing to wake up to."

"No shit."

"I got drunk that day."

"I only remember the morning."

"I only remember the night," Jimmy says.

"I went to school that day. It was like chaos on campus. I couldn't believe it, America was attacked."

"I spent the night at the bar, I got so drunk. I remember pissing in the urinal, crying for America."

"I cried that night too, I couldn't help it, I was scared," I say.

"You knew after that day, America would be changing."

"America has turned into an Arab-killing monster."

"I didn't want to be in America anymore after that day. I wanted to leave the country, but I never did, I stayed right here. Fighting the American war."

"Someday America will fall like Rome."

"America is Rome."

"Bush is Caligula," I say.

"I feel bad for those young kids fighting in this war. They don't know why they're there. They don't have a clue what's going on. It's not their fault they're not intelligent enough to not take orders."

"But that's who they are, they're people who take orders."

"I guess you're right."

"I'm happy that I'm in a strip joint at this moment. There's no better place to be for the beginning of a war."

"Yeah, it was a good idea to come here," Jimmy says.

"I'm not happy to be alive at this moment. There's something disagreeable about being American and human at this moment."

"I feel really discontent. Like there's something I should be doing. Like taking part in an anti-war protest or being over there in Iraq killing people. I don't know which one, but I feel like I should be doing something instead of getting drunk in a strip joint. But this is all I can do to support my country."

"Maybe we should sing 'The Star-Spangled Banner.'"
"Okay, let's do it."
"No, fuck it."
"Okay."
"Maybe we should pray."
"Okay, let's try it."
"How does one pray?" I say.
"Don't you have to believe in God to pray?"
"I don't think so."
"No, I'm pretty sure you do."
"Oh," I say.
"Well, what should we do?"
"Let's get more lap dances for the troops."
"That's a great idea."
We sit there frowning.
The redhead and China come back over.
We get more dances.
We both get hard-ons again.
The girls walk away.
We sit there rotting.
As we get older we are slowly learning.
That we can never control our environment.
That we are powerless.
That no matter how hard we try.
Nothing will ever get accomplished.
But we're like all humans, and we keep on trying.
It's compulsive.
It's human to be human.
We are like all artists and we think that if we create the perfect piece of
art, that suffering will stop, that the human war will end.
But it won't.
The human war is ceaseless.
As long as there are humans.
There will be war.
We don't get along.
That's why we drink.
Because we can't stand other humans.
Alcohol makes people tolerable.
Or very intolerable.
For violent drunks.

I think I'm going to spend the next couple of weeks drunk watching war coverage.

I'm going to sit drunk.

Watching the false reports.

And bullshit.

My friends will tell me I'm stupid for watching it.

But I won't care.

I'll watch anyway.

I will unwillingly succumb to the media.

Media.

Media.

Media!

The media controls us all.

Without the media there is no civilization.

Someday I will kill the media.

I'm going to kill it with a kitchen knife.

You watch.

It'll be historical.

Mark Swift kills the Media on November 10th, 2022.

Civilization will collapse.

The monkeys will break out of their cages at the local zoo and take us over.

Then there will be the monkey wars.

America will lose.

Because Russia will sell helicopters to the monkey warriors.

We will all die.

It'll be great.

Everyone dead.

Lying all over the place.

It'll stink.

But the monkeys won't care.

They won't even bury us.

They'll throw us all in the ocean.

And let us rot.

Absurdity.

Jimmy and I head to the bar for crapieoke.

Crapieoke is karaoke but with drunk kids in their early twenties and late teens at a piece of shit bar in Youngstown.

In the car I listen to the war reports.

It sounds sinister.

Death.

Bombs dropping.

Blowing up.

Then rubble.

I wonder what my children will think of this war.

Bush is a madman.

He doesn't care about anyone.

He and Nixon could be best friends.

America, when will you vote for a decent person.

I'd like to ask America a lot of questions.

But I don't even think they know the answers anyway.

I get to the bar, and go in.

The bar is on a shitty back street.

I go into the bar and stare at all the freaks who go there.

All the outcasts from Youngstown and Warren go there.

Goth kids, punks, indie kids, painters, skateboarders, and musicians.

A bunch of shitfucks basically.

I go and sit at the bar.

I order a Black Velvet and Coke.

I sit there in my own world, enjoying the view.

The war isn't on the television; it's some comedy show.

Everyone is laughing hysterically.

I'm in my own personal hell.

I rub my eyes and shed a tear.

And then Missy comes over and sits next to me.

Missy is this beautiful short-haired brunette.

I love her dearly.

She's a painter and reads Rimbaud.

If she would allow me, I would marry her.

"What's up Mark?" Missy says.

"Oh, nothing, getting drunk," I say.

"That's all one can really do in this time of crisis."

"You got that right."

"But I don't want to talk about the war. I can't handle it."

"I can't handle it either."

"Today is my last day at work," Missy says.

"Why, what are you going to do for money?"

"I have another job working for a make-up company. I sell make-up to old rich women for thirty dollars an hour."

"That sucks."

"No, it's all right."

"I hear you graduate this year. What are you going to do for the big job?"

"Nothing."

"Nothing?"

"Yeah, I don't care, I don't even know why I got the degree. It's a fucking painter degree. What can I do with that?"

"Go to New York and be a star," I say.

"Fuck New York, I'd rather stay here and be a big fish in a little pond."

"But you'll never make the money you could in New York."

"I don't want New York, I like my life in Youngstown."

"I wish I could say the same thing."

"Why do you stay here?"

"Because I'm mad and poor."

"That's a good reason," Missy says.

"Someday I'll leave and become great."

"You probably will one day."

"Yeah, I'll be a superstar."

"Don't forget me."

"I won't."

I look at her face and imagine her in a white wedding dress walking down the aisle.

"I'm writing a screenplay about restaurant life. See, I've realized how our generation has deeply depended upon restaurants to make money," Missy says.

"Yeah, I've thought of that. I've worked in at least ten restaurants and I'm only twenty-two. Our parents never worked at restaurants, they worked at the factories."

"Yeah, the restaurant is like our factory."

"There's also telemarketing, and door to door sales."

"Yeah, our generation has a completely different world of work opportunity than even people fifteen years ago."

"Our generation doesn't have much opportunity at all."

"No, it doesn't... Most of us have given up anyway. Look at this bar, these are all middle class white kids, and most of them will never finish college, they will just work shitty jobs, and get drunk."

"I hate to say it, but that's me too."

"It's me too, but I'll have a college degree."

"This world doesn't want our generation."

"No, and we don't want this world," Missy says.

"The world will be polluted to hell, and overpopulated when we get it."

"And the economy will be a piece of shit."

"I don't think the economy will ever rise again. And the Middle East will just get more and more fucked up. And the terrorism won't stop until we take our bases out of there, and leave them the fuck alone."

"No, we're fucked and that's all there is to it."

"And nobody even knows it."

"And no one even cares," Missy says.

"Hopefully we'll figure it out before it's too late."

"Hopefully... Well, I have to go tend the bar in the back. I'll see ya."

"See ya."

There she goes, the woman I want to marry.

I sit alone again.

Facing the universe.

I drink another BV and Coke.

Tasha sits down next to me.

Tasha is a notorious slut.

I've had sex with her, of course.

She has a big white ass.

That is so lovely.

She suffers from mental illness.

I had to visit her in the mental ward two weeks ago.

They should have given her shock treatments.

"How are you doing, Mark?" Tasha says.

"I'M FREAKING OUT!"

"Why, what's wrong sweetheart?"

"THE WAR!" I scream it for everyone to hear and look at me.

"I know, it's killing me too."

"THAT MONGREL PRESIDENT, I'LL FUCKING KILL HIM!"

"Calm down, get a hold of yourself."

"I WILL NOT GET A HOLD OF ANYTHING!"

I order another BV and Coke.

"Mark, it'll be all right."

"THERE'S A WAR ON, NOTHING IS ALL RIGHT!" I scream again.

"Mark, settle the fuck down!"

"NO, I'M FREE AND I WANT MY OPINION TO BE HEARD!"

"You won't stop the war acting like this."

"FUCK THE WAR AND THAT FASCIST BUSH!" I'm still screaming.

"Listen you're drunk, I think you should stop drinking."

"I can't stop drinking, I have to suppress my anger somehow. I think I'm going to start a fight," I yell at the crowd in the bar. "Is anybody Republican in here. Because if you are, I'm gonna fucking kill you!" Nobody responds, they just go on with their conversations.

"Come to the back of the bar with me and have a seat. Okay?"

She leads me to the back room of the bar where crapieoke takes place.

There are lazy boys from the seventies in the back.

She sits me down.

I fall into the chair, drunk.

I stare at the mongrels called humans.

I don't like them.

All of them are for the war.

All of them want my kind and me dead.

The dirty mongrels!

I notice that Tasha is wearing a sexy skirt.

I get the urge to fuck her.

Or punch her in the face.

I'm not sure which.

I get up and get another BV and Coke.

I walk around bumping into people screaming, "STOP THE WAR MOTHERFUCKERS!"

Everybody just stares and laughs.

But I'm fucking serious.

It's not that I don't think the causes for the war are just or unjust.

I just don't want fucking war.

I tumble into Jimmy.

I grab him by his shirt.

"STOP THE FUCKING WAR JIMMY, STOP THE GODDAMN WAR!"

"I can't Mark, this is beyond our control," Jimmy says.

"NO, STOP THE FUCKING WAR!"

Then I stumble away.

I keep gulping my BV and Coke through the straw.

I can no longer control myself.

I have to find a ride home.

I walk over to a really stupid hot girl and whisper, "Can you help me?"

"Yeah, what do you need?"

"I need to stop the war."

"I can't help."

"No one can," I say pathetically.

I stumble on.

I go back to the bar and get another BV and Coke.

The war has started in my mind.

Bombs are crashing into my neurotransmitters.

George W. Bush is talking in my mind.

Spitting beautiful lies.

I'm so tired of lies.

I seek truth.

But there is none to be had.

I want to go to sleep.

Humans are such vile creatures.

They deserve this war.

They deserve to die.

They deserve to have their family members die in the sands of the Middle East.

They don't care about anyone, not even themselves.

I no longer want to be human.

I walk amongst them like they're animals.

Because they are.

Animals.

Complete and total mongrels.

Mongrels.

All of them.

I will wage a personal war against them all.

And they'll love it.

Humans love humans who hate other humans.

Like Kurt Cobain.

He made a living off of hating people.

I sit in my cushioned seat, drunk, staring at the people in the bar.

It's their fault this is happening.

It's everyone's fault.

We are all part of America and its world domination.

We have no choice but to take part in it.

We don't know any better.

Like a dog who shits on the carpet.

Oh no.

The world and its madness.

Music is blasting.

A thousand bad conversations are taking place.

I'm stuck in the middle taking it all in.

Drunk.
Wanting to be dead.
America.
I lay back my head and close my eyes.
The room is spinning.
The dead walk among me.
Poetry is heard in the distance.
I think I might die tonight.
Here in this seat.
I don't see why not.
What do I have to live for?
Fifty years of being a drunken loser.
Fuck it.
I'll die.
Fuck!
I can't die.
What's happening?
I'm surrounded by humans.
The filthy monkeys.
I notice Tasha's friend Nicole sitting near me.
She's cute.
With pink hair in pigtails.
Pierced eyebrow, nose, and tongue rings.
She turns me on.
She begins talking to me.
I don't understand what she's saying.
I want her to shut up.
She says the phrase, "Will you fuck me?"
I don't know what to do with that phrase.
It sounds inviting.
I hesitate for a moment.
I've never fucked during a war.
I say, "Yes, but I don't know if I can get it up."
She says, "All right."
"Can you drive me home? I'm drunk," I say.
"Yeah, Emily will drive you home, and then I'll bring you back to my house."
"That sounds great," I say.
We stop talking.
Now I have to fuck someone.

That sounds terrifying.
This night is madness.
I think I have to go to the bathroom.
I stand up and wobble a little.
Then I slowly move toward the bathroom.
There are a lot of mongrels in the way.
I can't stand these people.
What are they doing in my way?
They shouldn't be there.
I finally make it to the bathroom.
I lock the door and crawl to the toilet.
I put my face in front of the bowl.
And then.
Vomit!
It comes out easy.
The world is collapsing down on me.
I can't stand the weight.
I don't need this.
I did this to myself, but I was compelled.
The last chunks of vomit come out pretty rough.
I think I might die in this bathroom.
And no one will ever find me.
Until I start stinking.
Then they'll open the door.
And find my dead body.
Rotting.
I stand up and head back out.
The people are still there making noise.
I can't stand noise at this point.
I think I'm blacking out.
I probably won't remember this.
I sit back down.
And pass out.
There is silence in my mind.
I'm at the bottom of the Grand Canyon.
There are pretty clouds hovering in the sky.
The sun is out.
It's seventy degrees.
I'm sitting with two Tijuana prostitutes.
We're drinking margaritas.

I'm happy.

There's no war.

Everyone is at peace.

God loves us.

There's real hope here.

America doesn't exist.

Saddam Hussein went to counseling, and he's a good person now.

George W. Bush got a tutor and learned the alphabet.

I put my feet into the Colorado River.

It's cold, but peaceful.

I feel at home here at the bottom of the canyon with my two prostitutes.

I wake up fifteen minutes later.

Noise!

The universe is a bloody cunt.

I feel less drunk.

Which is good.

I go to the bathroom again.

In there.

I shit.

It's hard shitting while you're drunk.

Trying to wipe is really hard.

My reality is mangled and distorted.

And there's no way out of it.

I go outside.

And sit on the grass cross-legged.

I light a cigarette.

And stare at the stars in the sky.

But they give me no solace.

The really hot girl comes out for a breath of fresh air.

She says, "Are you all right."

"Yeah, I'm fine, just a little drunk."

She sits down next to me.

"You look like you are going to cry, what's wrong?" she says.

"The war, it's tearing me up inside."

"Yeah, me too."

"It is?" I say.

"Yeah, I hope we get Saddam."

"What?"

"I want this war. Saddam is a horrible person. And Iraqis need to know what freedom feels like. It's pretty selfish for America to keep freedom to

themselves, don't you think?"
 "I guess."
 "Well, I have to go back in. See ya."
I sit there confounded.
I don't know what to make of this war.
I don't know what I should do.
I'll just be drunk.

The Doomed

In the local mental ward sat two humans.

Each lying on his bed.

David was fat and unattractive.

Jimmy was attractive and disturbed.

"Do I look ugly?" David asked.

"No, you look great," Jimmy said while reading a book.

"Because I think I look ugly."

"Why do you care so much?"

"Because I look ugly, do I look ugly?"

"Do you think you look ugly?" Jimmy said.

"I don't care what I think. I want to know what you think."

"I think you're a beautiful man."

"You do, really?"

"Yeah, you're a great-looking man."

"But do you think I'm ugly?" David said.

"You believe in God, don't you? Do you think He thinks you're ugly?"

"I don't know. Do you think God thinks I'm ugly?"

"I don't think He cares."

"Why wouldn't He care if I'm ugly or not?"

"Well, I would think He had more important things to dwell on."

"I don't know what He would dwell on besides my ugliness... Do you think I'm ugly?"

"No, I think you have a wonderful face. It's very symmetrical."

"You think?" David said.

"Oh yeah, it's marvelous."

"My mother's dead."

"She is? How come?"

"Her heart stopped beating."

"That must have been tragic," Jimmy said while still reading.

"It was. She was my best friend."

"Your mother is watching you from heaven. That's what dead people do, they watch us, even in the shower. I won't even masturbate because I think dead people are watching. They watch all the time. Every moment of the day, there's a dead person watching."

"My mother sees me lying here in the mental ward."

"Yeah, she's watching right now. She even watches when you shit."

"I don't want my mother to know I'm here."

"She knows, and she's crying a tear in heaven."

"Do you think I'm ugly? I don't want to be ugly."

David got up and walked in front of Jimmy's bed.

He stood there retarded and drunk-like.

"No one does. It's horrible to be ugly. I'd rather be pretty than smart any day."

"You would?"

"Yes, of course. Why would anybody want to be smart? It's such a hassle, knowing and understanding things. Intelligence causes suffering, but being hot, that just gets you laid."

"I haven't been laid in three years," David said.

"That's sad. You should save up and go to a prostitute. They're very convenient."

"I would never do that. I believe in God."

"It's obvious God doesn't care about you, so I don't see why you wouldn't."

"But my mother would be watching."

"You're right, she would... Why don't you go to a bar and meet someone?"

"I get nervous around girls."

"I get horny around them."

"Do you think I'm ugly?"

"I don't trust my own thoughts, so I'm not going to answer that."

"Please answer?"

"No, I refuse. You answer it."

"I can't, I'm not you."

"No, you're not. But I no longer trust my own thoughts, my thoughts don't make sense anymore, I'm always thinking something I don't want to be thinking, but I think I want to think. Then I think what I'm thinking is right and true, but then I think of something else that contradicts that, then I think some more, then I take pills and cry."

"Yeah, but do you think I'm ugly?"

"No, you're beautiful. Seriously. Sit down, you're making me nervous."

David went back to his bed and lay down.

Jimmy kept on reading.

"They put me on new pills," David said.

"How's that working out?"

"I'm nervous."

"So am I, but then I touched myself while thinking of the Rocky Mountains."

"Sometimes I touch myself."

"Good, don't tell me about it."

"I'm nervous."

"So am I, it's unbearable. I'll have to eat today, go to the bathroom, I'll probably shit, and then I'll have to wipe my ass. It's such a burden to exist. There's a lot a person has to do to get through the day, and I have no interest in doing any of it. Why can't I be left alone? I don't want to wipe my ass, it's disgusting. Don't you think it's grotesque."

"No, I enjoy it."

"Of course you would, you're fucking sick."

"I'm not sick. The doctor says I'm normal, but do you think I'm ugly?"

"I like the doctor, he gives me pills. Some people say depression is all in your head, but I'm like where else would it be, in your foot... People are delightfully annoying... Do you like people? Because I sure as hell don't."

David stood up on his bed and scratched his bulbous tummy.

"I'm fat. You think I'm fat?" David asked.

"No, you're like Adonis," Jimmy replied.

"I'm like Adonis?"

"Yes, you're a Greek god, David."

Melissa walked into the room and sat down on the edge of Jimmy's bed.

She was short and attractive.

"I got out of bed today," Melissa said.

"You did, that's beautiful," Jimmy said.

"Yeah, I'm real proud of myself."

"You should never exalt yourself."

"The doctor says I should be proud."

"The doctor is a madman. He lies to small children."

"No he doesn't, he's an honest man," Melissa said.

"Don't believe him. He walks among the dogs."

"What dogs?" Melissa asked.

"The devil dogs of the black forest," Jimmy replied.

"I doubt the doctor ever goes near a forest. He lives in Youngstown."

"So does Jesus."

"Jesus doesn't live in Youngstown. He lives in heaven."

"No, Jesus is a crack addict named Tyrone who lives in the projects. He drives a Chevelle instead of a donkey."

David still stood on his bed.

"I'm afraid," Melissa said.

"Of what?" Jimmy said.

"Of the day. The sun is out. There's light. Maybe it's time for our cigarette break."

"Ten minutes till cigarette break. I can't wait, I'm so excited."

"Do you think we'll ever get out of here?"

"Don't know, don't care. I don't want to go back out there, I'll have to get a job and function. In the mental ward, you don't have to function. It's great."

"I know. I like not functioning. It's peaceful," Jimmy said.

"We're wild humans. No one wants us out there."

"I had a job six months ago, I worked at Taco Bell."

"How'd that go?"

"The boss said I was doing a bad job, so I threw a taco at her head."

"Did it hit her?"

"No, it missed."

"That's sad."

"Do you think I'm ugly, Melissa?" David said.

"No, you look good, David," Melissa said.

"Do I really?" David said.

"Yeah, do you want to have sex?" Melissa said.

"Can we?" David asked.

"You're retarded, Melissa," Jimmy said.

"I haven't had sex in over a month," Melissa said.

"Why do you have to be such a whore?" Jimmy said.

"I'm not a whore. I'm a good girl."

"There are no good people," Jimmy said.

"My mother is a great person," Melissa said.

"Every time your mother comes in, she tells you you're fat."

"I love my mother."

"Your mother is evil, evil I say, evil!"

Melissa jumped on top of Jimmy and began punching him.

Jimmy threw her off.

"Take that back!" Melissa yelled.

"Fine, your mother is not a crazy bitch. She's a completely normal human being."

"Thank you."

"There are cameras everywhere. They're watching you right now. Do you feel them, caressing your skin?" Jimmy said.

"You're paranoid, there aren't any cameras. It's all in your head, Jimmy. You're a putrid little monster."

"I love you so much my balls hurt."

"You love me, don't you? You want to have my babies, I know you do."

"I want to anally rape you."

"I knew it, you loved me."

"I love our Lord and Savior. I'm married to Our Lady," Jimmy said.

"You're not married, Jimmy. You're a loser, a loser!"

"No, I'm a winner actually. I graduated from college with a three point eight average. You didn't even go to college. You sat around being a drunken whore while I worked my ass off."

"I couldn't go to college, I was too embarrassed."

"I want to hold you. Come here."

"No, you're a buttfuck. You make me feel like a loser."

"You are a loser."

"I'm a good person."

"So is my asshole."

"I help the homeless."

"The homeless are drunk."

"Unlike you, I do nice things for people."

"You don't even listen when people talk!" Jimmy said.

"I'm listening to you right now."

"No you're not, you're waiting for your turn to talk."

"You're a fucking asshole. All day you sit in your room reading because you think you're better than us."

"I like to read and I don't like talking to people."

"You're talking to me now," Melissa said.

"Because you came in here, I'm obligated."

"Do you want me to leave?"

"I want you to love me, I want to share a house with you, I want to grow old with you."

"No you don't. You just want to have sex with me."

"What's your point? As long as you're getting attention, you don't care."

"Shut up. Why can't you be nice? You're always so mean and vulgar."

"Lick my nuts, lollipop."

"Do you guys think I'm ugly?" David said.

"No. Sit down. You're making me nervous," Melissa said.

David lay back down.

"My mother is dead," David said.

"We know, you've told us a million times. Get over it!" Melissa said.

"She's watching you, David," Jimmy said.

"Shut up, Jimmy. His mother is not watching him," Melissa said.

"I thought you believed in God. Didn't you tell us all one day that he was coming back, and everyone but you was going to go to hell?"

"He is coming back, and you're going to hell when he does, Jimmy."

"Jesus isn't coming back, and I'm not going hell," Jimmy said.

"Oh yes you are. People like you go to hell."

"What kind of person am I?"

"A mean one."

"I'm a goddamn saint compared to you."

"I think you're possessed by devils. My pastor said that some people get possessed by devils and that's why they become mentally ill."

"I'm not possessed by shit. You're ridiculous."

"My pastor is right. Everything he says is true," Melissa said.

"Your pastor is an idiot."

"You're a turd."

"You're a dirty monkey sinner."

"I'm not a monkey. God created me."

"God didn't create shit, even God knows that."

"God created the world in six days."

"God lay around and smoked weed for seven days."

"You're an evil monster!"

"I'm pure of heart."

"Fuck you, I'm leaving!"

"Thank God!"

"Do you think I'm ugly?"

*

Jimmy, Melissa, David, and George sat in the smoking room.

George was a man in his early thirties.

"I love smoking. It reminds me of the desert," Jimmy said.

"You've never been in the desert," Melissa said.

"I live in the desert, see that cactus," Jimmy said.

"What cactus?" George said while looking around.

"Do you guys think I'm ugly?" David said.

"Yes, David, you're a monster," Jimmy said.

"Are you serious?" David asked.

"He's kidding. David, I find you very attractive," Melissa said.

"Quit leading him on!" Jimmy said.

"Shut up, Jimmy. You're a mule cock fucker!" Melissa said.

"I took a shower today," George said.

"How was that?" Jimmy said.

"I think I forgot to turn on the hot water," George said.

"Beautiful," Jimmy said.

"I want to go home, but my parents don't like me," Melissa said.

"Don't go home then. Go to the desert," Jimmy said.

"I'm already in the desert," Melissa said.

"Walking alone," Jimmy said.

"Yes, and forever," Melissa said.

"You can stay at my house," George said.

"You live in a group home," Melissa said.

"I do?" George said.

"George, what happened to you?" Jimmy asked.

"My mother raped me repeatedly when I was little," George said.

"That's horrible. You should kill her," Jimmy said.

"I tried when I got older, then they put me in the mental ward," George said.

"Where's my gun?" Melissa said.

"Why do you need a gun?" Jimmy said.

"So I can put George out of his misery. It's obvious that he's doomed," Melissa said.

"We're all doomed," Jimmy said.

"Yes, we are," Melissa said.

"Do you think we will ever see natural sunlight again?" George said.

"We would have to be let out for that to happen," Jimmy said.

"I'm leaving today, I know it," Melissa said.

"But where will you go? You've pissed off everyone you've ever lived with," Jimmy said.

"I will walk to the desert."

"The desert is three thousand miles away."

"I have a good pair of shoes."

"My mother died, I saw her die, they pulled the plug, and there she lay, dead. My mother, my mother!" David said.

"Did your mother ever stick her finger in your asshole?" George asked.

"No," David said.

"I'm not dead," George said.

"No, you're not. You should be proud."

"I'm proud to be alive," Melissa said.

"You're also a whore," Jimmy said.

"I'm not a whore," Melissa said.

"How many people have you had sex with?" Jimmy asked.

"Around forty," Melissa responded.

"How old are you?" Jimmy asked.

"Twenty-one," Melissa said.

"You're a whore," Jimmy said.

"I'm not. I'm a good girl."

"You are the death of God," Jimmy said.

"Shut up, Jimmy. At least I've had sex," Melissa said.

"I've had sex, just with people I loved," Jimmy said.

"You're incapable of love. You don't have the ability to create bonds with people," Melissa said.

"I will one day, I know I will," Jimmy said.

"I was in love once. She had the most beautiful smile in the world," George said.

"What happened?" Jimmy said.

"I shot at her, so she left," George said calmly.

"Why the hell would you shoot at someone you loved?" Jimmy said.

"She was always eating my food," George said.

"Good reason," Jimmy said.

"My father shot at me once," Melissa said.

"How was that?" Jimmy asked.

"I cried for a long time," Melissa said.

"Sometimes I cry when I think of you, Melissa," Jimmy said.

"Why would you cry for me?" Melissa asked.

"I cry because I feel sorry for you, because I love you," Jimmy said.

"You love me?"

"Yes, I do. I find you charming," Jimmy said.

"Ah... Maybe someday I'll give you a blowjob."

"I can only hope."

"I haven't had a blowjob in over three years... But I never liked them anyway," George said.

"I told the doctor I wanted to be free, so he gave me more medication," Jimmy said.

"Is it helping?" Melissa said.

"I don't want to be free anymore," Jimmy said.

"What do you want to be now?" Melissa asked.

"Drunk."

"I was drunk when they brought me here. I drank a bottle of whiskey, then I went to Denny's, and picked up everybody's cups in the smoking section and threw them at this picture on the wall of this one man walking alone in the desert. Then I got up on the counter and took off all my clothes. Then I think the cops took me here," Melissa said.

"What were thinking about when you did it?" Jimmy said.

"I was thinking about the time my dad threw me into the wall for spilling a cup of Kool-Aid," Melissa said.

"Why'd you take off your clothes?" Jimmy asked.

"I was going back to the primitive," Melissa said.

"One time I stayed out in the woods for three days, until my parents found me and sent me here," Jimmy said.

"One time when I saw my mother at the store and she said hi to me, I went home and cut off my pinky toe. Look, I have no pinky toe," George said.

"That's fucking grotesque," Jimmy said.

"You're deranged!" Melissa said.

"Do you guys think I'm ugly?" David said.

"Shut up, monkey!" Jimmy said.

"No, you look good, David," Melissa said.

"What do you think, George?" David said.

"What, where, who, why, when?" George said.

"Do you think I'm ugly?" David said.

"I don't think about you, David," George said.

"What do you think about, George?" Jimmy said.

"Right now I'm thinking about when I went to the Marines, and I was doing push-ups. I had to do so many, it was unbearable. I was in Desert Storm, I killed people. It was horrifying. I think about those people a lot too... About their families, if they had kids, if they're in heaven or not. I think a lot about those men... I killed people," George said.

"Well, you had to do it... If you didn't do it, then Kuwait wouldn't be free," Jimmy said.

"What do I care about Kuwait, I didn't even know the country existed before they sent me there... And it sucked there too. It was completely impossible to find a prostitute," George said.

"But you should be proud. You fought for America," Melissa said.

"I fought because they paid me," George said.

"I was little during Desert Storm. All I remember about it was those yellow ribbons everywhere. How come we aren't putting up yellow ribbons for the soldiers who are going to fight in Iraq?" Jimmy said.

"Because no one believes in this war... I certainly don't, I'm a pacifist," Melissa said.

"You're also a whore," Jimmy said.

"A whore can be a pacifist," Melissa said.

"Only in America," Jimmy said.

"I killed people," George said.

"Do you think I'm ugly, George?" David said.

"Shut up, David. The only reason you say that is because you want attention. And no one is going to give it to you anymore. So go fuck yourself," Jimmy said.

"Fuck you, Jimmy!" David said. Then he got up and ran out of the room, crying.

"Thank God that piece of shit is gone," Jimmy said.

"You're fucking mean, Jimmy. I'll never love you," Melissa said.

"I'm honest," Jimmy said.

"During high school I had sex with my best friend, Joey Smith... He had a huge penis," George said.

"I've had sex with men too. There's nothing wrong with that," Jimmy said.

"I've had sex with over ten girls. I love the softness of girls so much, but I love dick, and I can't leave it," Melissa said.

"You're absurd," Jimmy said.

"Shut up, fag," Melissa said.

"How can I be a fag, and yet love you?"

"Because you're deranged!"

"I'm not deranged. I'm a normal, well-adjusted individual," Jimmy said.

"I can hear you masturbating in your room," Melissa said.

"I do it for you."

"I think I love you, too."

"When we leave here, do you want to drive to Las Vegas and get married?"

"Oh, that would be perfect."

"I got married once in Mexico to a prostitute. Her name was Leonore, she was a beautiful girl... She wanted to go to America, and work at a hotel as a maid. So we got married and came to America. We lived together for a while, and then she left after I pulled a knife on her and said I would kill her if she ever ate all the ham again," George said.

"You have a way with women, George," Jimmy said.

"Did you ever have a relationship where you didn't try to kill the girl?" Melissa said.

"Once I was going out with this girl Jesse, she had the hugest tits... She left because one time she got really drunk and passed out, and when she woke up her asshole hurt like hell," George said.

"You're fucked up, George," Jimmy said.

"I'm a Marine, Semper Fi," George said.

"I think I'm going to try to kill myself today," Melissa said.

"That sounds like a great idea. I tried yesterday with a shaving razor, but they caught me before I was done," Jimmy said.

"I've tried to kill myself eleven times, and I can't die. It's starting to get frustrating," Melissa said.

"I'll get my dad to bring his muzzleloader when he visits, you'll be dead for sure then."

"Yeah, I need a gun. A gun would do a great job."

"Guns are really good at killing people," Jimmy said.

"I killed people with a gun," George said.

"You shall not kill, that's a commandment," Jimmy said.

"I know, I'm going to hell... When I die, I shall meet the devil," George said.

"When I die, I shall meet Jesus," Jimmy said.

"Jesus wouldn't go anywhere near you, you dirty fiend," Melissa said.

"I'm holy," Jimmy said.

"You're impure, and retarded," Melissa said.

"I have walked the length of the desert to get to my Christ," Jimmy said.

"I want to die and never wake up. No more reality, no more, no more," Melissa said.

"We're just skeletons... Underground we will lie, while the world is still going on. Then one day civilization will be gone, and then, there will be no one to remember the great and horrible things humans have done," Jimmy said.

"Quit being so depressing... My doctor says we have to think positive," Melissa said.

"Yes, let's be optimistic," Jimmy said.

"Someday we will get out, and we will be able to achieve our dreams, and be great citizens of America."

"Yes, one day, life will be beautiful... Life will be worth living, and we will live it."

"At one point in my life I was sitting in the desert shooting at people I didn't know, for a reason I didn't know... At another point in my life my own mother was fondling my penis... At another point in my life I was married to a Mexican prostitute... And currently at this point in my life, I don't even know what day it is," George said.

Bedroom Scene

In memory of Ashley Dixon. This was written several years before she ended her life. RIP.

During the cold Ohio winter, two people finished having sex. The boy's name was Jack and the girl's was Angela. They lay naked under the sheets of a single bed. The room was small. Earlier in the week, Angela had experienced a panic attack, and clothes and other shit remained scattered throughout the room. Jack was in his early twenties. Angela was nineteen. They were both attractive in an unexceptional way. They talked while smoking cigarettes.

"So we did it," Jack said.

"We needed it," Angela said.

"I didn't. Not tonight."

"Men always want it, whether they know it or not."

"Not me. I'm looking for love," Jack said.

"You don't want love. You can't handle being around anybody for more than a couple days. You get tired of people. The second you find love, you'll move on."

"You're no better," Jack said.

"The last boy I dated, I dumped him when he said he loved me. Just right there, on the spot, I broke it off. I don't need that shit. I'm young."

"But it gets lonely at night."

"You would think if you felt lonely, you would just go to sleep and forget about it. No, you stay up and dwell and dwell and dwell. I don't get to sleep until ten in the morning sometimes, the way it eats at me."

"That's what winter does. It eats at you. So we dwell in loneliness."

"I'm tired of dwelling."

"I'm on medication and it's not helping. I still dwell."

"Life wouldn't be so bad if you didn't have to be somebody."

"I wake up at five in the afternoon, go to Denny's, and just sit there until I feel tired enough to sleep."

"I get up every morning and get stoned, or take pills or something. Anything to make me forget."

"There is too much to forget."

The night collapsed down on them and they held each other close, as if afraid of something in the dark.

"I forget sometimes," Angela said. "Then it returns and I'm trapped."

"I was once a strong person. I went to college. I had a good job. I saw both oceans. To think now of all the time I wasted with Cindy. My god."

"Did you love her?"

"I think I loved her. Anyway, it's over now."

"Let's talk about something fun."

"When I was little, my dad used to take me to the batting cages. I always enjoy that memory."

"I don't have good memories like that. I never knew my father and my mom never did anything but bitch me out. My good memories came later, and it seems like every time I was happy, I was on drugs."

"I used to do drugs."

"How come you don't anymore?"

"They make me feel guilty. Guilty and like the world's a desolate place."

"I could spend the rest of my life high."

"I don't know how I want to spend the rest of my life, but I know I don't want to spend it high. Maybe everything I do is a mistake. Maybe I'll always be lonely. But drugs just make the loneliness worse. I don't want to make any more mistakes."

"I thought we were going to stop talking about sad shit."

"When I look back on this winter, I know that I'll laugh at myself. Right now, though, sad shit is all I feel."

"But then one day you'll snap out of it."

"One day I'll snap out of it."

"Doesn't the medication help at all?"

"I don't know. During the day, all I can really do is eat. Anything more is too much trouble. Is that helping?"

"All I can do is eat and get stoned."

"That's more than I can do."

Jack and Angela embraced. They kissed each other on the lips. Then she lit another cigarette and he got out of bed and went into the bathroom.

As he pissed, he wondered why he fucked her. He never had the urge to fuck her before.

Why tonight.

Is this love.

He flushed the toilet and returned to the small bed and climbed under the covers.

"You know what I did today?" Angela said.

"Woke up and got stoned."

"I watched PBS for five hours."

"Why did you watch PBS?"

"It's the only channel I get. I can no longer function without PBS. I can no longer function in the real world."

"Neither can I."

"I would like to be a real person and do real person things."

"The real world isn't worth it."

"But before I die, I want to see the world get at least a little better," Angela said.

"The world isn't going to get better. It'll be a shithole till the end."

"There's no truth anywhere."

Jack got out of bed and sat on the floor cross-legged. Angela pulled the covers up to conceal her breasts. They remained silent for a minute.

"I like having sex with you," Angela said.

"Thanks. You're not so bad yourself."

There was another silence. The small room was becoming intolerable to Jack.

"I saw my mother today," Angela said.

"Did you fight with her?"

"We don't fight anymore. She still tries to control me, but we don't fight anymore. She knows I'll start breaking shit if she yells at me. She's moving away, too. She's moving to a sunny place and I'm going to die here in poverty, alone. It's fucked up."

"I don't know what to say."

"Why can't you be like a normal boy and tell me everything is going to be okay?"

"I don't really know you all that well. I don't know if it will be okay."

"You're right. You don't know me."

Jack took a cigarette from the pack on the floor. He put the cigarette in his mouth but didn't light it. Angela stared at him. She let the covers fall, exposing her breasts, and she stared.

"Are you going to light that?" she asked.

"I don't know," he said, tight-lipped so the cigarette did not fall from his mouth.

"What if I said I loved you?"

Jack found a lighter and lit the cigarette, slow and deliberate, as if to postpone answering the question for as long as possible. Finally, he said, "You still have a chance to stop."

"What the fuck am I supposed to do?"

"Do something for yourself."

"No one does anything for themselves. People do it for their parents, to make other people think they're great, to get laid or make money, but they don't do anything for themselves. I don't have anyone to impress and there's nothing I want. I don't care about making anyone happy. I don't care if I'm happy. People can go fuck themselves. And that includes you and me."

"That's a good attitude. You'll get real far in life acting like a total bitch," Jack said. He stood and walked around the room, gathering his clothes.

Angela looked at him as if she wanted to say something, but she said nothing.

Jack zipped up his jeans and buttoned his shirt. He had worn his socks during sex, so he did not have to put them on now. He slipped on his shoes.

Angela was still looking like she wanted to say something.

Jack considered saying goodbye. He thought better of it.

Why tonight.

Is this love.

He walked out of the room and left through the front door, ducking out into the cold night to his car in the driveway, where he sat. He felt the same as he did before he fucked her, only somehow crueler.

Back in the house, Angela lay in bed. She screamed and howled out to the night, but there was no one there to listen.

Little Flowers

1

My dad brought me to the train station.

It's a rainy night.

I've just graduated college with an English literature degree. I've never traveled in my life. The farthest I've ever been from home is Virginia Beach.

I'm sitting in the train station in Youngstown, Ohio, reading. I look around the room and see a fat white trash woman eating Taco Bell. A Chinese girl and a white guy cuddling, and a lonely woman reading a romance novel. It's a sad sight.

It's two in the morning.

I've lived a stupid life. My college existence consisted of going to bars and sitting at Denny's till sunrise. I've had several girlfriends for long periods, but I don't know if I have loved any of them. I said 'I love you' to them, but I probably just said it to get laid.

I've lived so many useless days. Days I can't even remember.

The train arrives.

Everybody stands up.

We all march out to the train and get in.

It's dark and everybody is sleeping.

A conductor takes my ticket, and I sit down.

I put my luggage up in the rack.

I'm nervous about this trip. I'm not one for adventure. I'm not one to live his life to the extreme. I'm boring. I graduated in four years. What kind of normal person does that?

I'm alone.

No one is here to help me.

No one is here to keep me safe.

I have to do this all by myself.

I've never done anything all by myself.

I'm not a loner.

I've just always wanted to be one of those guys who does insane things, has insane adventures, and just lives a really cool life.

I guess this is my chance.
I fall asleep.

2

I wake up in the morning.
The train is moving toward Chicago.
I look around the train looking for somebody to ask where the lounge is.
There's an older man with a ponytail. He has a stupid look on his face.
But I ask anyway. He answers, and then I go to the lounge.
I walk to the lounge and get a coffee.
I ask where the smoking section is.
The worker says there's no smoking on this train.
I'm very pissed.
So I go to the bathroom and smoke a cigarette.
It sucks smoking in a bathroom.
I realize I'm not at home anymore.
I'm afraid of that fact.
I walk back to my seat.
Drink my coffee and stare out the window. There's nothing out there.
Just ugly land.
I see a lonely cow in the distance.

3

The train arrives in Chicago. I get off the train into this huge train station.
I don't know where I am. I don't know where to go. My reality is hard to
comprehend.
I walk out of the train station after looking for the way out for ten
minutes.
I stumble down the street looking for a coffee shop.
There are none.
So I go to Starbucks.
It's no smoking there.
I order a plain coffee and sit down with a book.
I read and sometimes look out the windows at passersby.

The coffee is too hot, and it tastes horrible.
The people of Chicago look pretentious.
They all look like poets and politicians.
I look homeless compared to them.
I finish my coffee and head back on the town.
I stop a taxi and take it to the library.
We ride around town for a little bit and he drops me off.
I walk up to the door.
And it's closed.
The taxi is gone.
I get another taxi and go back to the train station.
I don't know anything about Chicago.
I don't know where to go.
I don't feel safe just walking the streets aimlessly.
I'm afraid of missing my train.
Even though I have five more hours till I have to get on it.
I get back to the train station and eat.
I have a shitty cheeseburger.
Now I only have four more hours to go.
So I decide to get drunk.
I go to the bar and start drinking.
I drink rum and Cokes.
The world is slowly becoming a better place.
A young girl is sitting next to me.
She's pretty. She has short blonde hair, a nose ring, and tight clothes
on. So I start up conversation.
    "Hi, what's your name? I'm Arkady," I say.
    "Hi, my name's Lucy," she says.
    "How come you're at the train station?" I say.
    "I'm going to New York."
    "Wow, that's cool."
    "I don't feel like flirting. Let's talk," Lucy says.
    "Talk about what?" I say.
    "Your mother."
    "My mother, why?"
    "I'm not interested in boring conversation," Lucy says.
    "Okay, what do you want to know about her?"
    "How did she treat you as a little kid?"
    "She was at work most of the time, I never really saw her."
    "Is she vulgar?"

"Yes, very vulgar."

"Does she fart in front of you?"

"Yes."

"Do you spend time with her now?"

"Well, I smoke with her in the morning at the kitchen table. We usually talk then."

"Do you tell her about your sex life?" Lucy says.

"Yes."

"I don't have a mother."

"You don't?"

"No."

"Why did you want to hear about mine?"

"I like to try to imagine what it would be like to have a mother through other people's mothers."

"That's weird."

"I don't care if it is weird. I do it, all right."

We sit there for a minute in silence.

"Why are you going to New York?"

"To read poems at cafes. All I've ever wanted to do was read my poems at cafes. I don't care what job I have, it could be the shittiest job in the world, I just want to read my poems."

"That's a beautiful dream."

"You think? Why are you traveling?"

"Because I just graduated college, and I want to see America."

"America ain't all it's cracked up to be."

"I don't know, I just want to do it."

"I guess you have a dream just like me."

"I'm going to just sit here and get drunk. That's my plan."

"I have to get on my train in fifteen minutes... I suppose I'll see you later."

She gets up and leaves.

I just sit there and drink.

A fat man with a beard sits next to me. He looks like a hick from somewhere out in the country.

"Hey kid," he says.

"Yeah, what do you need?" I say in a drunken voice.

"Ever hunt for bear?"

"Nope."

"I have, it's fun as hell. I shot one too, and killed it. They make great burgers."

"They do?"

"Yeah, they make great burgers."

"I killed five bunny rabbits with a pellet gun once."

"You did, how'd you do it?"

"I ran around the yard shooting them until they died. My neighbor paid me fifteen dollars to do it."

"That's cool. I should try killing a bear with a pellet gun."

"I don't think it would work."

"Neither do I."

"I used to kill birds too. One time I killed a rooster."

"A rooster? Why'd you kill a rooster?"

"It pissed me off."

"Yeah, my rooster pisses me off too."

4

Eventually I get on the train.

I'm drunk as hell.

The train is slightly crowded.

There's a fat woman talking about her well-adjusted grandkids.

I want her to shut up.

I talk to no one.

I've never been good at striking up small talk.

Actually I hate small talk.

I also hate people who talk small talk.

The lounge opens up.

They have two-dollar whiskey sours.

I run down there and buy one.

Then I go to the smoking section.

The smoking section is almost full.

There's every race of the world in it.

We're all smoking for America.

A guy in his fifties wearing a beret covered with military pins is sitting in the corner of the smoking section. He keeps flirting with a Mexican girl who doesn't understand English.

The girl just sits there smiling.

I'm drunk and I don't care about anything.

I get up and walk around the car.

No one is paying attention to me.

I sit back down.

I start talking to an Asian woman next to me.

"Do you love yourself?" I say.

"No, I hate myself," she says.

"Why do you think about yourself so often then."

"Because I don't care about other people."

"Neither do I. I try to care, but I can't," I say.

"It's not worth caring too much about other people. You have to just let them go."

"I know, you can't change anybody. And you can't make them happy."

"Humans are goofy, but they're also cruel," she says.

"I know, they're animals. I'm one of them, and I don't know anything about them. Fuck it."

I stand up and go back to my seat. I sit there for a long time.

Years pass as I'm sitting there.

I eventually get up and go back to the lounge.

I wobble down the aisle.

I order another drink and sit at a table.

An old man sits near me.

He says, "Who are you?"

"I'm me."

"That's convenient."

"No, it's frustrating."

"Do you suffer?"

"Of course."

"Someday you'll die."

"I believe it," I say.

"There's no God."

"Perhaps."

The old man stops talking.

I drink my whiskey sour.

I'm exhausted.

I go to the smoking section for one last cigarette.

I sit down and look at all the animals.

There's a young girl with dreads.

I reach out and hold her hand.

She looks at me and smiles.

The Condemned

THE WARRIOR

In a small rented house.
    Kathy sits on her couch.
    Eight months pregnant.
    She bends over.
    Using a rolled up dollar she sniffs a line of coke off the coffee table.
    Her belly protrudes.
    Kathy is beautiful.
    Five ten, long legs, soft skin, thick lips, large blue eyes.
    The body and face of a movie star.
    Kathy's four-year-old runs through the living room.
    She looks at him.
    Stares.
    Looks angry.
    Kathy gets up and sprints at the boy.
    Smacks him straight across the face.
    The boy flies into the wall.
    The boy does not cry.
    He crawls to his bedroom.
    The boy looks scared, that is all.
    Kathy goes back to the couch.
    A small woman named Lisa is sitting too.
    Lisa says, "What's with that whore Judy, fucking bitch, goes home with a different guy every night."
    "She's a fucking whore, what can you say," says Kathy.
    "At least five men come into the bar every night, she talks to them, then they leave. It's bullshit, that damn strip joint is a fucking whore house."
    "Most strip joints are whore houses, Lisa."

"That ain't fucking right."
Lisa sniffs a line.
Kathy sniffs a line.
The television is on.
Jay Leno is giving his Monday Headlines.
Kathy and Lisa sit back and watch.
"I love Leno's Monday Headlines," says Kathy.
"Yeah, so do I."
Kathy gets a notebook and pen.
She begins to write to her boyfriend in prison.

Dear Joe,

You are a fucking asshole. I hope somebody butt-fucks the shit out of
you. I hope they butt-fuck you so hard your guts fall out of your asshole. I
hope you piss off the blacks and they shank you with a toothbrush.

Love,
Kathy

*

Kathy is at work.
Eight months pregnant.
She is a stripper.
The bar is small.
Grungy.
Men usually go there alone.
Miserable men.
Men who work hard.
But can't figure out why they work so hard.
They are divorced.
Their children are in other states.
If the men were not there.
They would be sitting at home.
Watching television.
Alone.
Most make around sixty thousand a year but have no one to spend
their money on.
So they go to this strip joint in Youngstown.

And give their money to the girls.

Kathy is sitting next to a man named Chris.

Chris works construction.

He works hard.

He's sunburnt.

Has several tattoos.

Lives in a small apartment.

He had a wife, but his wife, who people say was a wretched bitch, got pregnant but not with Chris's baby.

They got divorced.

He hasn't been laid in five months.

"You are really beautiful," Chris says to Kathy.

"Why, thank you," says Kathy.

Kathy puts her hand on Chris's knee.

Chris feels her hand on his knee and enjoys it.

He hasn't been touched by a girl in so long.

To him, her hand touching his knee is as big as actually fucking.

Chris smiles at Kathy.

The song is about to end so Kathy asks, "Would you like a dance?"

"Yeah, of course."

Chris moves his chair around.

Kathy stands up and dances.

She rubs her butt on his crotch.

Chris puts his hands on her legs.

They are so long and soft, he thinks.

Kathy smiles during the whole dance.

She knows what lonely men want most is a smile.

The legs are good, the tits are good, the ass is good, but it's the smile they love most.

The dance is over and Chris hands her five dollars.

She gives Chris a hug and a kiss on the cheek.

Kathy walks away and sits by Viper, another dancer.

Viper is a blonde white girl with a big ass.

She is an exhibitionist and doesn't do drugs.

"You know what Joe called me today when I went and visited him? That son of a bitch called me a fuck twat."

"A fuck twat?"

"Yes, a fuck twat!"

"How come?"

"I told him about how I fucked Ed, but I only told him that because he said this baby in me ain't his."

"What an asshole."

"That's what I'm fucking saying! Where the fuck is Dave, I need some shit. This is bullshit. He said he would be here at 10:30. It's like 11:15."

"Hell, I don't know."

"How are things going with you and Lenny?"

"Good. He offered to buy me a car the other day, but I told him no," says Viper.

"Are you serious?"

"Yeah."

Another dancer named Micky comes over.

Micky is overweight, constantly high on Oxy, and drinks half a bottle of Crown a night.

Micky says, "I lost my car last night. Do you guys know where it is?"

"Are you fucking stupid? How the fuck did you lose your car?" says Kathy loudly.

"You know," says Micky in that slow Oxy voice.

"I don't give a shit. Get away from me," says Kathy.

Micky walks away.

A few songs pass.

Kathy gets up and goes over to a man.

His name is Bob.

He wears glasses and has bipolar disorder.

Kathy knows what must be done to get twenty bucks for two songs from him.

She starts dancing.

She strokes his dick behind her back.

Kathy turns around and lifts her leg up, pulls her panties over gracefully.

Bob touches her pussy with his finger.

Bob looks up at Kathy.

Kathy smiles.

Kathy is wet.

So Bob's finger goes in easy.

On the second song Bob decides not to finger her so much and rubs his hands all over her pregnant belly.

Which makes Kathy giggle.

She loves when people notice that she is pregnant.

Kathy puts up her leg.

Bob sticks a twenty in there.

*

Kathy, age four.

 Coloring on the floor.

 Her mother sits in a chair drinking, sporadically sniffing a line.

 Kathy colors everything red.

 She has only one crayon.

 Kathy's mother looks down at her.

 Stares at her.

 Sweat is on her mother's face.

 Her eyes boggle about in her skull.

 Her mother licks her lips.

 She pets Kathy's hair.

 Kathy looks up at her.

 "Yes, Mommy," Kathy says, scared, knowing that if Mommy pays attention to her it is only to punish her.

 "Come sit on Mommy's lap, Kathy."

 Kathy gets up and sits on her mother's lap.

 Kathy is covered in dirt, wearing a dress.

 Her mother begins to kiss her on the lips, and sticks her tongue in Kathy's mouth.

 Kathy kisses back because she thinks Mommy finally loves her.

 After kissing for a while Kathy asks, "Mommy, why did you kiss me? You've never done that before."

 "Well, no man will because your stupid ass is here."

*

Kathy gets home from work.

 Sits on the couch.

 No lights are on.

 Silence.

 She thinks, I would like a strawberry.

 Happiness is important at 3am.

 Lights off.

 Drowning in silence.

 Darkness.

 Broken and shivering.

 Goosebumps.

 Fear and trembling.

The hours pass.
Kathy is afraid to move.
Movement leads to failure.
Choices build castles.
Castles have ghosts.
The ghosts now come to Kathy.
Man with a mullet and rebel flag tattoo.
And a big boot.
On Kathy's small head.
Pushing and pushing and pushing.
Down.
Onto concrete.
Pain.
She feels the pain.
Kathy trembles.
Grabs her hair.
Pulls at it.
There is ugliness.
Strong punch to the face.
Kathy misses Joe's punches.
They hurt so much.
Black eyes.
She has scars.
Knocked out twice.
Ambulance.
Police.
The guns.
Her mother.
And television.
And school teachers.
And the behavior of a thousand generations of women.
She is a woman.
A woman cannot be intelligent
A woman must be weak.
A woman must breed.
Beget the next hopeless generation.
She hears sounds.
Sentences that contradict.
Women must get beat.
Big dumb tears on her cheeks.

Choices build castles.
Castles have ghosts.
Kathy goes to the kitchen.
Pours some Crown into a coffee mug.
Goes into her bedroom.
It is small.
Without pictures.
Without any decorations at all.
She lies down in the small bed.
Rubs her belly.
The baby kicks hard when she's tweaking.
Kathy drinks the Crown and falls asleep.

*

Lisa walks through the door.

"Bitch, where's my motherfucking money?" screams Kathy.

"For what?" screams Lisa.

"For the fucking phone bill, what the fuck do you think? I'm fucking putting you up when you ain't got no place to fucking live. I need my fucking money!"

"I only made fifty-five dollars last night."

"What the fuck? You go home with that guy for free last night? What the fuck you do that for? He would have fucking paid you."

"Hmm."

"Hmm, is fucking right bitch, just give me what you have."

Lisa gives her thirty-five dollars.

"Thirty-five dollars, I thought you made fifty-five you lying bitch, where's the rest of my money?"

"I need twenty for tip-out."

"Fine fucking whatever! But whatever you make tonight, I get that too."

"All right, Kathy."

Lisa takes Kathy's orders.

Lisa's dude is in the pen also.

For shooting a crackhead who wouldn't pay up.

The man didn't die.

He just can't walk anymore.

Lisa is small, like four ten, and eighty-eight pounds.

Lisa is almost dead.

She has to be stoned or tweaking or drunk to even deal with the act of tying her shoes.

She is from somewhere down south.

Lisa says her dad is a millionaire.

When Lisa is drunk or tweaking or stoned she says that she has never seen her dad.

Lisa only dates black guys.

Nobody knows why.

There are many white girls like that.

And there are black girls who won't date black guys, but date any white guy who exists.

Here in Youngstown.

*

Kathy is sitting inside a restaurant.

Eating a burger with french fries.

She notices that there are pickles on her burger.

She'd asked for no pickles.

Kathy waves the waitress down.

The waitress comes over.

"Yes, miss, do you need anything?"

"Yeah, motherfucker, I need another burger, because this fucking burger has pickle juice all fucking over it!"

The waitress lies and says, "But miss, you didn't ask for no pickles."

"Listen motherfucker, I know what the fuck I said. I said no motherfucking pickles, so take this fucking burger off this goddamn table and get it the fuck away from me, and I don't wanna see your fucking face till I got a brand new burger without any goddamn pickles on it. And you better make a new one, and not just wipe off the pickle juice, because I will fucking check to see if there is any goddamn pickle juice on it. And if there is, there is gonna be some shit going down up in here. You know what I'm fucking saying, bitch?"

"Yes, miss. I'll fix it immediately."

*

It's the middle of the day.

Lisa is asleep on the couch.

Dismal light comes through the windows.

THE COLLECTED WORKS VOL. I

NBC is playing on the television; it is the only channel Kathy gets.

Kathy has all of her money out on the coffee table.

There are sixteen twenties on the table.

That is a lot of twenties, Kathy thinks, but not enough. I need more twenties.

Kathy reaches for the phone.

She calls Joe's dad.

Joe's dad works at Packard. He has money.

"Hello."

"It's me, Kathy."

"Oh, hi Kathy."

"Yeah, well, are you gonna help with this baby?"

"We aren't even sure it's Joe's."

"It's fucking Joe's, who the fuck else's would it be. You calling me a slut?"

"No, I ain't calling you a slut. We just aren't sure."

"Now, listen here. I don't fucking lie when it comes to things like babies. You know what I'm saying?"

"Yeah, but I think we should have a test."

"All right, after the baby is born. We'll have a fucking test. But I want this baby to be part of Joe's life. You know I didn't grow up with a father. I don't want my baby to grow up without a father. You know, what the fuck, this is important to me. But you know I need money to stay alive. I'm still working and I'm eight months pregnant. I need at least three weeks off to get this baby out."

"Yeah, I know. But we aren't sure."

"How long have you known me? Come on, I just need like a hundred dollars. I just got the electricity bill, and I don't know if I have the money to pay it. And I got to make repairs on the car, and all kinds of shit."

"All right, I'll see what I can do."

"Okay, that sounds great. I'll be right over to get it."

*

It is Kathy's day off.

She is sitting in her living room wearing a cornflower blue jumpsuit, with her make-up done up pretty.

There is a knock at the door.

It is her son's father.

His name is Eric.

He sits on the couch.

Eric is thin and looks like a skeezer.

"So I let you fuck me for a week, and you buy me a car, right?" says Kathy.

"Yeah, that's the deal. I'll give you two thousand dollars on any car you want."

"Any car I want."

"Yeah."

"All right. Do you have the shit?"

"Yeah, I got it."

Eric takes out a baggy of coke and dumps it on the table.

Kathy gets some Vicodin and crushes it and mixes it with the coke.

They sniff the coke together.

Kathy can't fuck unless she is tweaking.

Eric knows that.

After Kathy is plenty high.

She takes her clothes off.

And they fuck.

*

Kathy is at work.

Sitting with Viper.

Kathy says, "Viper, do you think I'm a whore for fucking Eric for the car money?"

"No, I don't consider it prostitution if you've fucked him for free before."

"That's what I thought too."

*

Kathy is seven years old.

She is in the car with her mother.

Her mother is tweaking bad.

They are driving down to the south side to get more drugs.

Kathy's mother is crying.

Kathy sits peacefully in the passenger seat.

Classic rock is playing on the radio.

Kathy's mother speaks to her, "You see Kathy, these bitches, they don't know any better. You know. Like your fucking aunt. She don't know shit. Yeah, she's a fucking slut. I think she owes me twenty dollars. I should kick her stupid white ass if she don't give it to me. Fucking bitch. I gotta get some more shit, Kathy. Mommy got it hard."

Kathy stares out the window.

Her mother always talks like this.

Kathy doesn't know what to say to it.

So she just sits there.

Her mother pulls into a parking lot.

Looks at Kathy and says, "Now listen you little bitch, you better be nice to Reggie. He's got the good shit. All right."

Kathy's mother puts her hand on Kathy's face.

Kathy doesn't smile.

She is silent.

Her mother pulls out of the parking lot and goes down a side street.

Inside Reggie's house, several people sit around, tweaking.

The people talk incessantly.

The conversation goes nowhere.

But still they keep talking.

Just a bunch of fucks, shits, and hells, and motherfuckers is all Kathy hears.

Her mother talks to Reggie.

She tells Reggie she has no money.

Reggie points at Kathy.

Kathy's mother says, "What do you want with her?"

"Just to touch her a little bit, that's all, I'll be happy to give you a hundred dollars worth," says Reggie.

"A hundred dollars worth?"

"Yeah, good?"

"One fifty."

"All right, one fifty."

Kathy's mother walks over to Kathy and says, "Now Kathy, I want you to go with Reggie, and be nice to him. I'm your mother, remember that, so do as I say. Now follow Reggie, and just be nice to him for Mommy okay."

Kathy looks up at her and says, "All right, Mommy."

Reggie and Kathy go into the bedroom.

Reggie does no more to Kathy than her mother does at night.

*

In the dressing room at work.

Kathy sitting on the counter.

Viper on the toilet, pissing.
Kathy stares at Viper peeing like she wants to eat her.
Viper notices her stare.
And stares back.
Viper says, "Kathy, you are so fucking sexy."
"Thank you. I think you're hot as hell."
Viper rips off a piece of toilet paper and wipes herself.
She stands and pulls her thong up.
They return to work.

*

Kathy is sitting with a customer at the bar.
He looks at her and says, "I would like to take you home, spread open those legs, and eat you like Thanksgiving Dinner."
Kathy looks at him, smiles, and says, "How much can you afford?"

*

Kathy is alone at work, in the bathroom.
She sniffs a line off the counter.
Then looks up at the mirror.
She puts her hands on her belly.
The baby is kicking hard.
She stares at her pregnant belly in the mirror.
Kathy thinks. Her thoughts are loud. Fuck, not another one! I can't take another one! Why won't this baby just die! Just fucking die! I already have one, and I don't even like that one! How the fuck am I supposed to deal with another one! Why won't you just come out!
Kathy punches her belly.
She squeezes it.
But nothing happens. The baby keeps kicking.
She sighs.
Her face melts in the mirror.
Ghosts come through the walls.
They are staring down at her.
Crushing her beneath their boots.
Rich faces.
Faces that have money look at her.
She must look down.

Happy faces.
Clean faces.
Faces untouched by the horrors of the world.
Look down at her.
She must look away.
For she is the filthy, impoverished trash of America.
America, where nothing can be wrong.
For America is always. For Americans are moral and good.
They set the world straight.
Kathy sets her twenties out on the counter.
She has seven twenties.
She lives for those twenties.
She has no bank account.
No savings or checking account.
No Visa or Mastercard.
Just those seven twenties.
She counts them.
Holds them in her hand.
And laughs about those stupid bitches who work in restaurants and retail who don't make shit.
She makes seven twenties barely working at all.
There is no time in Kathy's world.
No future, just a timeless present.
Her life only stretches as far as her twenties, and how she can spend those twenties.
Kathy stares at those seven twenties.
She adds up how many twenties it will take to feed her and her son.
How many twenties she can devote to bills.
Then she will know how much she can spend on coke for the evening.
Clocks and calendars, long terms goals, mean nothing to Kathy.
Only that she has enough twenties to get her to the next time she can get more twenties.

*

Eight months earlier.
Kathy is standing in her living room.
Screaming at Joe.
Joe is sitting on the couch.
Staring up at her.

Both are tweaking.

Kathy screams, "You are such a little man, such a little piece of shit. What the fuck is wrong with you, are you fucking retarded, I'm speaking to you, are you fucking retarded! Cuz, I think you might be. I think you might be fucking retarded. The verdict is in. Joe is fucking retarded!"

"Shut the fuck up, you stupid bitch!"

"You telling me to shut the fuck up, oh yeah, little man. You are such a fucking retard, Joe. You ain't shit, you know that! You's a little bitch, a bitch. Everybody said you were a bitch, and you know what now I fucking believe them. Bitch!"

Joe stands up.

Punches her in the eye.

Kathy hits the floor.

Joe sits on her chest and punches her in the face repeatedly.

Blood everywhere.

Kathy is still screaming, "Bitch bitch bitch, you's a fucking bitch!"

Joe keeps screaming, "Shut up shut up shut up!"

Joe stands up.

Kicks her till her ribs break.

Then grabs her by the head and smashes it into the floor.

Kathy eventually passes out.

Joe says quietly, "God, you're a fucking bitch."

Kathy lays there all bloody and stupid.

Joe leaves because he is on probation.

When Kathy wakes up.

She crawls to the telephone and dials 911.

An ambulance comes and puts her on a stretcher.

The cops go and pick up Joe.

He has just spent two years in the pen for shooting a person.

While arresting him they find enough coke in his car to convict him of drug dealing.

He is sentenced to eight years in prison.

*

Kathy is sitting across from Joe in the prison.

There is glass between them.

They are both holding phones.

Joe says, "Did you bring my money?"

"Yeah, I brought your fucking money."

"Good, it's because of you I'm fucking here."

"I'm not the one who kicked my fucking ass, dick head."

"You didn't have to call the police!"

"I was gonna fucking die, asshole."

"Fucking slut! Shut up!"

"I hope you fucking die in here. You know that! Our son doesn't need assholes like you in his life!"

Joe looks at her for several seconds.

He spits on the glass.

Kathy watches the spit slide down the glass and smiles.

*

One night after work, Kathy goes to Viper's house to spend the night.

Viper's house is small and old.

The kitchen hasn't been remodeled since the late fifties.

The furniture, tables, drapes, and appliances are all second-hand.

Her parents own the house; it was inherited from a dead great uncle.

There is a bookshelf with everything from Stephen King to Simone de Beauvoir.

Viper grew up poor like Kathy. But Kathy grew up outside the city of Youngstown, in a bordering town.

Both of their grandpas worked for the steel mills.

But Viper, unlike Kathy, had a father who was around when she was young.

She wasn't so unstable.

And her parents, unlike Kathy's parents, had an interest in her future.

They took out a loan for her to attend college.

Kathy is sitting on the couch and Viper is in the kitchen.

Kathy sits there rubbing her belly.

She is tweaking and the baby is kicking hard.

Viper yells from the kitchen, "Would you like a drink?"

"Yeah, I need something to calm me down."

Viper puts ice cubes in two tall glasses.

Fills the glasses almost to the rim with rum and then pours some soda on top.

She enters the living room and hands Kathy a glass.

Viper sits on the couch and crosses her legs.

Kathy takes a drink and smiles.

"You live here all alone?" says Kathy.

"Yeah, just me."

"How come you don't have any kids?"

"Don't want any. I would rather have a swimming pool."

"What?"

"Well, I like swimming more than I like kids."

Kathy doesn't respond.

She just sits there staring at her swollen belly.

After some time passes, Kathy says, "How's Lenny?"

"Good but he's getting a bit clingy."

"Yeah, he seems like he'd be that type."

"Yeah, but he eats such good pussy. I got this other guy lined up. Andre. You've met him before, he goes to the club on Thursdays."

"Yeah, he's hot."

"Yeah, I know. Strong as hell too! Uhh, that's what I'm talking about," says Viper.

Viper's sentences are like grenades in Kathy's head.

"You know, you're like a warrior. You go out and get things that you want. You tear it up. It's like when you enter a room, people take notice. You fight tooth and nail for what you get. I really like that about you," says Viper.

"I do, I have fought like a motherfucker for what I have. I just got a new car. I got all my bills paid. I still got my kid. I got my own place to live. I got it and for what I've done for it, I deserve it."

"You know people say that you have to go and get what you want out of life. But it isn't like that. It's like, the more money you make, the less you actually do. People say going to college is going out and getting it. But in reality it's just plodding along. I show up to class, they tell me to memorize these certain things. I do, then write in the answers. The whole process takes years. It's like that at work too. I worked at a toy store for two years and became a manager in my department. All I did was show up on time and take orders well, and never thought. Just did one little dumb thing after another. And somehow that leads to success."

"I worked at a restaurant once, but the manager kept giving me shit. So I punched her in the face."

"We do what we have to do."

"Ain't that the truth."

They sit on the couch in silence.

*

Kathy and her son pull into the Wal-Mart parking lot.

Kathy's son gets out and starts running around the parking lot.

The kid is making that siren noise only kids can make.

Kathy gets out, nine months pregnant.

She runs after him, screaming, "What the fuck do you think you're doing, you little fucker! Get back over here now!"

Kathy catches the little boy.

Begins smacking him.

Kathy screams while hitting him, "You little fucking piece of shit! I ought to fucking kill your little ass! What the fuck do you think you're fucking doing running around this fucking parking lot? You'll get hit by a fucking car! Then you know what? You'll be fucking dead, you little fucker!"

She is hitting him and screaming and the boy is crying.

A family loading groceries into their minivan stares, wondering how a woman could do that to her child.

Kathy looks at them and screams, "WHAT!"

*

Kathy is sitting with Viper at the bar.

Both just sitting there.

Sipping at their drinks.

Kathy looks off and says, "Now that Joe's in prison, I sit at home mostly. Watching TV, doing nothing. The other day I was in the store and I saw that there's Tide with a Touch of Downy now. Tide with a Touch of Downy. Things like that, they get me through the day. Tide with a Touch of Downy."

*

At work.

Two girls come in with a guy.

One of the girls is named Nicole.

The girls are wearing expensive clothes bought from magazines and off the internet. Clothes that are brand new but made to look old and faded.

Nicole sits down with her friend and starts talking shit about Viper and the dancers. "Look it's a bunch of skank Wal-Mart girls. Viper has a big ass, fucking slut." A lot of random dumb shit.

Viper is across the bar, out of earshot.

Kathy is a couple of seats down and hears everything.

Kathy stands and walks toward them and says, "Look bitches, you gotta fucking problem, what the fuck do you think you're doing coming up in here and saying shit about Viper. I think I might kick your fucking asses."

The two girls look scared but stupidity keeps Nicole talking, "Whatever, you white trash bitch."

Kathy, pregnant as hell, punches Nicole in the face.

Nicole falls off her seat.

Viper approaches the other girl from behind. She taps her on the shoulder. The girls turns and gets a right hook to the eye. The bitch falls beside Nicole.

The guy they came with stands there.

Kathy starts yelling, "Look at these high class bitches. You know where you are now, high class bitches. You in a fucking place you don't fucking belong! So get the mother fuck out!"

Viper then kicks Nicole in the ribs and giggles and says, "I don't take no shit from an upper class bitch."

The two girls eventually run out to the new cars their parents bought them and drive away to their safe neighborhoods.

*

Kathy and Viper are sitting at the bar drinking.

Kathy says, "Now that I know Joe ain't gonna be outta prison for eight years, I gotta move on. But I don't want no pussy boy, you know. He gotta be a man. If I get into some shit at the club I gotta be able to call him and say, 'Show the fuck up here now and be ready to kick some ass.' And even if we know we can't win, he still needs to come, and at least bring some heart, you know."

*

Kathy is twelve years old.

Sitting on her grandma's couch watching television.

Her grandma is sitting on a chair sipping on some vodka and Coke.

"Where's my mother?" Kathy says.

"She ain't here," her grandma says.

Kathy gets up and goes to the bathroom.

Sits on the floor and stares.

There's no use.

Kathy leaves the house and walks down to where a hotel used to be.

It is night.

The moon shines through the clouds sometimes.

The rubble is still there.

Broken cement scattered everywhere.

Other young kids are there.

Kathy sits on some rubble.

A young girl says, "Did you hear they burned down a crack house on Albert Street last night and another abandoned house caught fire on the south side last night."

A young white boy pulls out a joint and hands it around.

The children smoke the joint and get high.

Kathy says, "This is good weed."

The white kid says, "I stole it from my dad. He gets good shit."

The black girl says, "You living at your grandma's now, Kathy?"

"I've been there for two weeks now, and my mom doesn't seem to be coming back anytime soon, so I guess I am."

"I lived with my grandma for three years, but now I am with some fucked-up crackhead foster mother using my ass to get money. But she don't give a fuck what I do, so it don't bother me," says the black girl.

They sit on the rubble and wait for something to do.

*

Kathy is sitting in the living room watching television.

Lisa is sleeping on the couch.

Kathy has been sitting there for over an hour.

She stands up and punches Lisa in the back.

Lisa jumps up, looks scared, and says, "What the fuck you doing?"

"Where's my money bitch?"

"I don't have any, I don't even have tip-out tonight."

"Bitch, I need that fucking money to pay the fucking phone bill! If the phone goes off I can't talk to Joe. You owe me like a hundred fucking dollars bitch. Where's my fucking money?"

"I used my money on the drugs last night, remember?"

Kathy stares at her.

Kathy is very mad.

Kathy looks at Lisa and says, "You better have that fucking money soon."

"Whatever, just don't fucking hit me. I'm your friend."

Kathy just stares at her.

*

Kathy is two centimeters dilated.

She hasn't worked for a week.

She is alone.

There is an eight ball on the coffee table with some Vicodin mixed in.

She sniffs a line.

Then sits.

Her face is angry.

She looks at her belly.

Her large belly angers her.

She says, "I'm fat."

Then says, "Why won't you fucking come out!"

Then says, "Who the fuck is your father!"

Then says, "This is so wrong."

Kathy never cries.

But she cries now.

Some ugly tears fall out of her eyes.

She sniffs another line.

And stares at her belly again.

Kathy says, "You're gonna cry aren't you! You're gonna fucking cry constantly, and annoy the fucking hell out of me! You're gonna need to be changed! You're gonna need diapers, formula, clothes, all kinds of shit that I will have to spend money on. My hard-earned money will be spent on your stupid fucking ass! I lost so much by having the first one, now I will lose more. How much can you little fuckers take from me! All you little fuckers do is take! You give nothing but annoying grueling hours! You are cruel little monsters. I don't wanna teach your stupid ass the alphabet or how to walk or how to shit in the toilet. But if I don't take your shit, then my stupid fucking mother will take your shit. And that bitch is nuts! This is horrible!"

Kathy sniffs another line.

Looks at her belly again and says, "What will be your life, you'll be just like your father, you'll end up in the pen. You'll steal, sell drugs, you'll beat women, you'll throw it all away. But here I am with the plan of spending thousands of dollars on your ass making sure you live long enough to go to prison. That you live through eighteen shitty years in

Youngstown to end up in a little cell writing letters to some woman who ain't me. And she probably put you there, just like I put your father there. I don't want to give you life. I don't want you to know what it means to be poor in this world. What it means to be afraid! Really fucking afraid!"

Kathy sniffs another line.

She looks at her belly again and says calmly, "I'm bringing you into a world where you will know more people in prison than people who have graduated from college. You will know violence. You will know what it means to be hit and what it means to hit. You will know what it is like to wake knowing you have a better chance of getting into prison than getting rich. I will teach how to handle yourself in this environment. How to survive knowing that each day might bring violence and incarceration. I will teach you how to be as tough as steel and how to take no shit from motherfuckers. I will teach you how to get what you want. There is no reason to teach you the alphabet and read books to you at night. They ain't gonna help you here. Nobody cares about us and nobody ever will, we are poor people. We are doomed to this violence and struggle, and if I show you anything before you hate me when you get older, it will be how to survive in this hell."

Kathy sniffs a line.

She looks at her belly and says, "Education will make you a talker, not a doer. And nobody cares what the poor have to say anyway."

*

Kathy is giving birth.

She is gonna pop it out soon.

An anesthesiologist comes into the room.

It is a woman from India. She is there to administer the epidural.

Kathy screams, "Get this bitch out of here, I need somebody that can speak fucking English!"

The woman speaks; Kathy doesn't understand anything she says.

"Oh hell no bitch! Unless you get somebody in here that can speak English I'm walking down to St. Judes!"

Kathy gets up with the top of the baby's head about to be poking out, with her ass hanging out the back of the gown.

Kathy leaves the room and starts screaming, "You people are trying to fucking kill me, you motherfuckers are trying to kill me! Give me an American doctor, you people are trying to fucking kill me!"

They eventually find her an American and she has the baby.
It comes out normal.

*

In the hospital.
Kathy lies in bed.
The curtains are pulled back.
Stale sunlight comes through the window.
Hitting Kathy's pretty young face.
The baby is born.
The baby is without a name.
It is a boy.
Kathy doesn't know what to name him because she got into a fight with Joe. The baby was gonna be named Joe Jr.
Joe is saying he does not want to claim him.
Kathy's mother is holding the baby.
Looking at it smiling.
Pretending she cares about something besides herself.
Kathy's belly is finally empty.
She is relieved.
She stares at the baby her mother is holding.
That came out of my pussy, she thinks. That little thing came out of my pussy. That is so gross. But at least I am empty now. I can start getting skinny again.
Joe's parents come into the room.
Joe's dad is wearing a grease-stained white t-shirt. He has a foot-long mullet and is slightly bald.
Joe's mother is fat and has a dumb submissive look on her face.
Joe's dad looks at the baby.
They ask how she is doing and other stupid questions.
Eventually it leads to Kathy saying, "Are you gonna help with the baby or what?"
"We want to find out if it is actually Joe's," says Joe's dad.
"Of course it is, who the fuck else's would it be."
"We just want to make sure. The government will pay for it."
"He can either accept that it's his baby or he can fuck off."
"Fucking Kathy, I gotta go, this is bullshit."
"Good, get the fuck out. Don't take care of your son's baby! Assholes!"
Joe's parents leave.

Kathy says to her mother, "Motherfucking assholes, that asshole with his Packard job."

Soon after they leave, a Child Services worker arrives.

She is a fat woman who looks polite.

The fat woman says to Kathy, "We received a phone call saying that you used drugs while you were pregnant and that you beat your son. We are going to run a drug test on you. Would that be okay?"

Kathy looks out the window. She screams, "If I had a machine gun I would blow all you motherfuckers away! Why don't you fucking just leave me alone!"

Kathy looks at the Child Services worker and says, "Whatever, fucking do it."

A nurse comes in and takes her blood.

Her mother is still holding the baby.

Kathy hasn't looked at it once in the last hour.

*

It is the next day.

Kathy sits cross-legged in her hospital bed.

Lisa and Viper are there.

Lisa is holding the baby.

Kathy asks Lisa, "How much did you make last night?"

"Fifty-five dollars. It was a real slow night."

"That's bullshit, what are you fucking drunk all night. If I was there and all skinny I would be pulling hundreds out of those assholes' pockets. What are you, fucking stupid or something."

Lisa looks like she is going to cry.

Viper is eating a candy bar.

The Child Services worker enters.

Viper and Lisa have to leave.

The Child Services worker says to Kathy, "We found weed, alcohol, and cocaine in your blood."

"Yeah, so."

"Well, we are going to check up on you once a week for six months now."

"Oh, yeah. That sounds like fun."

"If we find that you have been using drugs or hurting the children, we are going to take your children away, just to warn you."

"You ain't gonna take my fucking kids away."

"This is a warning, I will be there every Wednesday at ten in the morning to check up on you."

"I'll be waiting. Tell my friends to come back in."

The fat woman leaves.

Lisa and Viper enter.

Lisa says, "What'd she say?"

"None of your fucking business, bitch."

*

Two weeks later.

Kathy is in her house.

The baby is in a crib, crying.

Her son is outside shoeless throwing stones at a neighbor's dog.

Kathy hasn't seen him in what feels like weeks. But she doesn't wonder where a small boy like him could go off to. She already knows the answer.

Kathy is sitting down trying to watch television.

She went back to work at the club last night.

She looks angry.

The baby won't stop crying. She yells at it, "Shut the fuck up, you little piece of shit! I'm trying to watch television."

Lisa walks through the door.

Without looking at her, Kathy says, "What the fuck you doing here, bitch? Where's my money?"

"I don't have it."

"Well, maybe if you weren't such a fucking junkie you'd fucking have it."

"Kathy, I'll get it to you."

Kathy motions for her to come close.

Lisa knows she shouldn't, that going close to Kathy will lead to something bad. But she goes anyway.

Lisa moves close to Kathy.

Kathy grabs her hair with her left hand and punches her in the face with her right.

The baby is still crying.

Then Kathy gets up and picks Lisa up and throws her out the door and yells, "Bitch, I don't wanna see your fucking face unless you have my money! You got that! I want my fucking money!"

Lisa is lying in the gravel driveway crying.

Kathy just stares at her.

She is fascinated by her crying.

Kathy walks back inside her house and locks the door.

Lisa is screaming like a small terrified child, "What the fuck am I gonna do, I got nowhere to go! I love you Kathy, please help me! I don't have a phone, Kathy! I took care of you and your boy while you were pregnant. I thought I was your fucking friend. You fucking bitch, Kathy!"

Kathy is sitting in the living room. She turns the television up.

Lisa stands.

She begins to walk down the street.

*

Kathy is at a guy's house.

His name is Randy.

Randy is seventeen.

He has short hair and is wearing a white undershirt three sizes too big.

Kathy has the baby and is showing it to him.

Randy is holding the baby and says, "You sure this ain't my baby? Because I would take a paternity test if you want. I mean, if it's mine I kinda would like to know."

"No, it's not yours. Don't worry. Isn't it cute?"

"You sure it ain't mine? We did have sex around that time, Kathy."

"Randy, what the fuck you talking about? It's Joe's. I know it's Joe's, so don't give me no shit."

"All right Kathy, it's Joe's."

"That's right. Now ain't he cute?"

*

It is Tuesday night.

Kathy is alone in her house.

She brought an eight ball home from work.

She also has a bottle of Vicodin.

She makes one big giant thing of powder with both of them.

Kathy begins sniffing like Al Pacino in *Scarface*.

The baby cries.

She screams, "Shut the fuck up!"

Then her boy runs out of his room and looks at her.

"Don't you fucking look at me!" Kathy says.

The boy looks scared but keeps on looking.

Kathy charges at the boy.

She punches him in the face.

"I thought I told you not to look at me, you little motherfucker! What the fuck is wrong with you? Can't you fucking listen?"

She continues to hit the boy.

Eventually she picks him up and throws him on his bed.

The boy is crying.

She goes into the living room and sniffs more and more and more.

Kathy gets through half of it in less than an hour.

She stands up.

Walks up to her entertainment center, which contains a television that can only get NBC and a broken CD player and some used movies. She knocks the whole thing over.

The baby cries louder.

Then she goes into the kitchen and throws the microwave at the floor.

Then rips the pictures of her and Joe off the wall.

Kathy punches the walls.

Putting little cracks in the drywall.

Then she goes into the kitchen and gets the bottle of Jim Beam she had under the sink from before she was pregnant and starts swigging from the bottle.

Kathy sits down in her chair.

The baby is crying.

Her boy is crying.

She finishes the bottle and smashes it against the coffee table and passes out.

*

It is Wednesday, ten in the morning.

There is a knock at the door.

Kathy looks up from her chair.

The baby is sleeping.

She walks to the door and opens it.

Kathy has a huge smile on her face.

There is some powder visible in her nose.

The fat woman looks at her like she is going to kill her.

The fat woman calls the police.

The police come and take Kathy away.

And they take her baby and boy away.
Kathy laughs in the back of the cop car.
She can't stop laughing.

*

The police don't keep Kathy for very long.
The prisons of Youngstown are too full.
So they send her home.
Without her children.

*

Kathy's mother calls her on the phone.
Kathy: "They took my fucking kids, those fucking assholes!"
Mother: "You'll get them back, don't worry."
Kathy: "This is what you fucking wanted from the beginning, bitch, isn't it. So you could have the fucking kids. No bitch, I'm not gonna let that happen!"
Mother: "Wouldn't it be better if they were with family?"
Kathy: "I don't give a fuck who they're with, as long as it ain't you!"
Mother: "I'm your mother, show some respect!"
Kathy: "All you deserve from me is your ass kicked!"
Mother: "This is your fault, Kathy. You're the fucking junkie, not me."
Kathy: "I should really just fucking kill you, shouldn't I. I should just drive down to your fucking house and rip your fucking head off!"
Mother: "I'm your mother and I love you."
Kathy hangs up.

*

Kathy is lying down on Viper's couch drinking rum and Coke.
Viper is sitting in an armchair, drink in hand.
Kathy says, "They took my man, they took my children, what else does this fucking world want from me. I want my fucking kids back. I ain't got nothing, Viper. Nothing. No kids, no man, barely any money. I only got one twenty on me. This is fucking bullshit!"
Viper looks at her and says calmly, "Do you need those kids? Do you need Joe? Or maybe a better question would be, do they need you?"
Kathy sits there and stares and eventually says, "You know if anybody

else would have said that I would have broken their nose?"

"I know."

"I don't know, I don't wanna be one of those bitches with their kids taken away. I don't wanna be like my mother. A shitty mother."

"So you're saying keeping those kids has nothing to do with kids. You're keeping them so you aren't one of the women who has their kids taken away and so you aren't like your mother, that's all."

Several minutes pass till Kathy says, "I don't fucking know. I hate people, I hate women, I hate men, I fucking hate everyone! What the fuck, what the fuck, what the fuck!"

"Yeah."

"But I'm Kathy. I'm tough-ass Kathy, and to be a tough-ass bitch, you need a tough-ass dude in the pen. And if he ain't in the pen, you just aren't as tough. But bitches know that if your dude is in the pen, you're fucking tough. And I'm Kathy who keeps her kids, who has them and still does drugs, and never lets them get taken away. I have my fucking kids!"

"You don't have shit!"

"You know, I would have killed you by now if you were someone else."

"Yeah, I know. But you came here for me to tell you this. You knew exactly what I was gonna say."

"Yeah, bitch."

Laughter.

"So since you don't have your kids anymore, you wanna move in and eat my pussy all the time?"

Kathy takes a big gulp of her drink, smiles, and says, "Yes."

Viper pushes down her pants and thong, points to her pussy and says, "Listen bitch, come over and lick my pussy before I beat your ass."

Kathy gets on her knees and crawls over to Viper.

Viper grabs her by the hair and smacks her across the face.

Then brutally pushes Kathy's face into her pussy.

GRATUITOUS KINK

THE IMMACULATE CHERRY POPPING

I lost my virginity in a church.

It was with a female named Taylor.

She was a big girl. Nice and round. With big baby cheeks.

Long brown hair and a shitty personality.

Something was wrong with her mentally.

She never told the truth. Was always stoned. And suffering from delusions of grandeur.

She had a rich dad and a white trash mom.

Her parents were divorced.

Her dad loved Jesus and big houses.

Her mom loved beer and weed.

They both sucked as people.

The church was big.

One of those evangelical churches on a back street that upper class white people go to.

The type of people who drive SUVs, vote Republican, and have portraits of Ronald Reagan in their living rooms.

The kind of church that has tambourines, dancers, live music, and tongues.

Actually the week before I lost my virginity I was anointed with the gift of tongues at the church. I was like, "Ekky, boo, shick, licky, me, tutu."

It was great, I felt really connected to the Lord. Yeah, just like that.

On some random Sunday when I was fifteen, I went to church.

I don't know why I was there.

Taylor probably invited me.

She always did stupid shit like that.

There isn't much to do on a Sunday morning anyway.

Which is probably the motivation behind most of the congregation.

All the assholes had piled into their seats and the service began.

I was sitting next to Taylor and she said, "This sucks, let's take a walk."

It sounded better than listening to some weirdo talk about how God condemns homosexuals, Jews, Muslims, Buddhists, Catholics, Mormons, people who have had abortions, people who have premarital sex, and the poor to eternal damnation.

So I said, "All right."

Why not?

So we got up and walked out of the service.

We went up some stairs.

Walked down a hallway.

She talked the whole time about shit that doesn't matter to anyone, not even her.

We went into a room with a piano.

She locked the door.

We weren't going out.

I didn't really even like her.

I think she loved me, but in a blockbuster movie scary kind of way.

She was like most people I've met. They only love people who won't love them back, because if they were actually in a relationship everyone would find out they're an asshole.

We sat on the floor.

She said, "You're really weird."

"Oh yeah," I said.

"My father is such a fuck head."

When she got to talking about her father, it didn't end for a while.

When people start bitching about their parents, you have to be prepared to hear a lot of strange and disgusting sentences.

She had the habit of analyzing everything they did wrong, and just stopping there. Never analyzing herself, just her parents.

I didn't care though.

I was too busy hating my parents to hate someone else's.

She eventually got around to the sex.

"Wouldn't it be cool if we had sex?" she said.

"In a church?" I asked.

"Yeah, that would be awesome."

"Hmm, do you have a condom?"

"Yeah."

Taylor reached into her purse and pulled one out.

She always carried condoms around like she was this big slut.

She used to talk about all the guys she fucked.

I never believed her.

Taylor had such a bad personality, the only person who would hang around her was a person who had absolutely no self-esteem and nothing to do. Like myself.

I've met a lot of young females who prided themselves on how many people they've slept with. Later I found out that they didn't sleep with half the people they said they fucked.

Usually those are the girls who have their self-esteem destroyed by their parents and don't have the motivation to do anything well, so they suck at everything. Sleeping with people is pretty easy; the only thing a person must do for that is show up.

"Do you think we will go to hell for having sex in a church?" said Taylor.

"Having sex in a church isn't mentioned in the Bible as a sin," I said.

"But sex before marriage is."

"Hmm, to tell you the truth, I don't really care. I wanna lose my virginity. Being a virgin is boring."

"I don't know, we might go to hell."

"Listen Taylor, first there would have to be a God. Second a hell, and third evangelical canon says that the Lord is All Powerful and that our lives are predestined. And that He has chosen who goes to hell and who goes to heaven before we are even born. So it doesn't matter what we do."

"You're right, let's do it."

Taylor was wearing a dress; she stood up and pushed her panties down.

I took off my pants.

Service was still going on.

All the assholes were still there listening to the pastor discuss a verse from the Old Testament.

One of the verses where God gets pissed and kills a bunch of sinners.

I got real hard.

Was excited.

Was gonna lose my virginity.

She told me to lie down on the floor.

I got down and lay there impatiently.

She got on top.

I saw that she had hair on her bush, but it was trimmed.

She put my dick inside her pussy.

Her pussy was nice and wet.

It slid in easy.

I was like holy shit this is sweet.

Not sweet like rose petals and Valentine cards.

But like Corvettes and the Cleveland Browns going to the playoffs.

I was high.

My dick was in a pussy.

And it felt good to be in that small compact area.

She pumped up and down.

Down and up.

Up and down.

She went slow, pretending she was making love to me.

I didn't care; my dick was in a pussy.

I had waited so long.

So long.

It was great fun.

So much better than my hand.

I came after three minutes.

It was an excellent three minutes.

My dick was in a pussy!

I felt so happy.

So fucking happy.

Don't know how she felt.

Don't know if she enjoyed it or what.

Never asked.

Was probably just another person she could tell people she slept with.

But sometimes that's the deal.

I give you attention, bragging rights, or money, and we have sex.

And it works the same way with males too.

Service was over.

Taylor needed to find her dad to get a ride home.

We walked out.

There were assholes everywhere.

I felt very happy.

Everyone kept saying how happy I looked.

They were right, I was delighted to be alive.

I had found my niche in the world.

I had found something to do, something better than smoking weed, playing video games, reading, drinking, being a good friend, and politics.

A real escape.

The impact of an orgasm on the human body and mind is the only experience that can remotely relieve the existence of all the bleak shittiness of human reality.

When I was fifteen, my life really sucked.

I was imprisoned in a house with a narcissistic mother who hated everyone, everything, and herself. And wanted everyone to feel the same as her.

My father was this typical Italian character who didn't speak and randomly beat his wife and kids.

Both my parents were non-theists. They didn't care a fuck about God or religion.

We said grace at Thanksgiving but that was just for fun.

That is probably why it was so easy to fuck in a church, because my parents showed no appreciation for religious values.

Which was fine with me, because after you grow up you realize that religious values are ownership, SUVs, hate, guilt and money.

Those values have no basis in reality and are totally boring and taxing.

I rarely saw Taylor after that.

We had sex in the woods a couple of months later.

It was on a beach towel.

I lasted a lot longer, probably because I didn't want to have sex.

It was obvious that her sexual motivations with me were psychological and not physical. It is hard to get it up when your function during sex is to give somebody a psychological fix.

DOWN IN MEXICO

The next few years of my sex life sucked.

I freaked out and had to go to the mental ward and a high school for the mentally ill.

The doctors put me on anti-depressants that killed the intensity of my horniness.

Actually, it killed everything I was.

The pills just made me numb. I was dead to everything for three years of my existence.

The only activities I had energy for were reading and masturbating.

I masturbated heavily during those years.

The internet had just come out; I worked at a fast food restaurant, saved up and bought myself a computer.

I got the internet and masturbated at least once a day.

It was hard finding free internet porn that would get me off back in the late nineties. It wasn't like it is today.

But I always persevered.

If it took two hours on my knees in front of the computer, I would do it.

I would search and search and search for that one pic that would excite me enough to get me off.

My knees hurt badly, but the physical sensation of an orgasm was more important than the pain in my kneecaps.

Sex in high school was lame, as it is for everybody.

I usually lasted three minutes.

I feel so bad for females in high school.

I've heard it said by females that sex doesn't really start feeling good until about the fifth minute, so if the males never reach the fifth minute they probably think, "What the fuck am I even here for?"

While I was in the school for the mentally ill, I had a short affair with my counselor.

I went to her house a couple of times and made out. But it never came to anything.

It was real weird; I was still in my jumpy excited sex stage.

She was thirty-one and in her let's make sweet love stage.

It was botched so we never had sex.

My sex life didn't really start until I graduated and got off those damn pills.

I went to the Grand Canyon to work the summer after I graduated.

Lasted at the Grand Canyon for a month.

They fired me so I went to San Diego.

Met some ass named Paul.

He was living in a hotel I worked at.

I would work the midnight shift and he would tell me all these strange stories about Tijuana.

He talked a lot about prostitutes.

I was really horny. So I listened.

Once, on my day off, I went to Tijuana.

Rode the trolley there from downtown San Diego.

Walked through the human suffering to get to Revolution Blvd.

A lot of men were yelling at me to buy their sisters and crystal meth.

I walked on.

Paul told me to go to a place called Bambi's.

I was very focused on getting laid, but I noticed I was in a complete hellhole.

There were children everywhere asking Americans to buy gum and bracelets.

The sun was beating down on the faces, concrete, and beggars.

I was sweating heavily.

The cab drivers were yelling at me to get a ride from them, so I did. I said, "Take me to Bambi's."

The cab ride was hell, everyone was beeping and there was a parade for Vicente Fox.

The cab driver dropped me off in front of Bambi's.

I handed him a five even though it was a two-minute ride.

There were two men standing by the door. They were yelling at every American that walked by, "TITTIES, PUSSY, TITTIES!"

They opened a curtain for me and I went in.

The place was dark, verging on creepy.

There was a stage in the middle of the room with seats around it.

A female was dancing. She looked cute.

A man came over and led me to a table.

Then the man asked what I would like to drink in English and I said, "Tecate."

He brought the beer back and put his hand out for a tip. I gave him a dollar.

The waiter left.

I sat for three minutes and a girl came over.

She was ugly and I didn't want to have sex with her.

She put her hand on my crotch and said, "You wanna go to a motel?"

I responded, "No, just give me a minute. I'm relaxing for right now."

She said, "Okay." Then left.

Another dancer came over. She was medium height and really hot.

She had on tight stretch pants and a tight shirt.

She had a pretty face and soft black hair.

She said her name was Liticia.

Liticia put her hand on my crotch the same way the other dancer did and said, "You wanna go to a motel."

It became obvious that was one of the few English sentences they could say.

I said, "Yes, let's go."

She grabbed my hand and we walked out of the bar, down the street, then down a side street.

We got to an ugly motel that rented rooms for one hour at a time.
I paid for the hour's time.
We went into the room and she asked for thirty dollars.
I took it out of my wallet and gave it to her.
She looked beautiful standing there.
I was horny and very lonely.
Hadn't even touched a female's body in over four months.
Was dying to just touch someone.
She said we had an hour.
I wanted that whole hour.
Liticia and I lay on the bed together.
She let me take off her shirt.
I touched her skin.
It was so soft.
I liked touching it.
She removed her bra.
She had perky little titties.
I kissed them and put her nipples in my mouth.
Liticia removed my shirt and ran her hands over my chest.
There was no talking; neither of us knew the other's language.
She didn't allow kissing.
She removed my pants and boxers.
She put my penis in her mouth and sucked.
She was a real pro.
Not like the females back home.
Liticia knew what she was doing.
I pushed her pants off of her.
She had on a tiny black thong.
We rolled around together in bed.
Nakedness against nakedness, it was so nice.
I felt so good just touching another human.
It is so rare that humans get to touch each other.
Soon enough we got to the fucking.
We were doing it missionary.
I noticed her hand was over her genitals.
I had heard stories from Paul about how some of the prostitutes were male.
I put my hand down there and looked at her.
While still pumping.
Liticia looked scared for a second.

I had several choices at that moment.

1. Get pissed and split.

2. Get all homophobic and beat the shit out of her.

3. Say fuck it, suck some Mexican she-male cock and get fucked in the ass.

I said, "Me gusta Jotos," which means I like she-males.

She smiled and lifted her hand.

There dangled a half-hard uncircumcised penis.

I pulled out of her and sucked it.

I didn't see why not.

I had never sucked a penis before and thought it was about time.

It was sweaty.

I gagged a little.

It got harder and felt weird in my mouth.

It felt like a rock wrapped in pig intestine in my mouth.

The pleasure came from the dirtiness of it, not from the actual act.

Maybe I would have enjoyed it more if it was bigger and circumcised, but you take what you can get for thirty bucks.

Liticia seemed happy about the whole event.

She asked in gestures if I wanted to be fucked in the ass.

I had never been fucked in the ass before, so I knew it would hurt.

The only object that had ever been in my ass besides shit was my middle finger, and her dick was much bigger than my middle finger.

I was a bit scared to be impaled by a penis, but still, it was about time.

Liticia went to her purse and got another condom, put it on herself and got on the bed.

She positioned me like a piece of meat.

I felt very objectified.

It was obvious that Liticia had done that before.

She had seen many Americans figure out she had a cock, or actually choose her because they figured she had one. And wanted to be anally penetrated and controlled by her.

I repeat, she was a pro.

Lititicia didn't have any lubrication on so she just spit on my ass.

Which was really sexy.

I bent over doggy style and waited for insertion.

I looked forward at the wall, sweating.

Her dick entered my rectum.

PAIN, REAL FUCKING PAIN!

I took it like a pro.

The pain eventually went away and I started to enjoy it.

I stayed hard the whole time I was being pumped.

She ejaculated into the condom—that was on her dick—that was in my ass.

Then she allowed me to fuck her again.

I was so happy.

I blew a huge load.

It almost killed me.

I fell out of her.

Lay there on the bed half-dead.

There was slobber running down my chin.

Liticia got off the bed, went to the bathroom and washed off her dick.

I went into the bathroom and she handed me the soap to wash mine off.

The both of us stood there, me a Youngstown boy, and her a really hot Mexican chick with a dick.

It was weird.

But the best experiences always are.

We put our clothes on and left the motel.

I walked down the street thinking about how awesome a fuck that was.

I went to a bar and drank some Tecate.

I sat there staring.

Ordered some food.

Ate it.

A man came over with a guitar and asked if I would like a song played.

I handed him some money and said play something miserable.

He did.

THE ASIAN SPA

I decided to go to the Asian Spa.

There are Asian Spas all over the Youngstown area.

I drove there nervous as hell.

I think I had the music turned down I was so nervous.

I parked in the back and went through the front door.

Then came to another door that you have to buzz.

An older woman came to the door.
She asked me how old I was and I told her twenty-one.
She asked to see my ID.
I showed it to her.
She let me in and led me into a small room with red lights, a twin bed, and a wall made of mirrors.
She told me to take off my clothes.
I did.
I was nervous.
What weirdness was going to come?
I sat naked on the bed.
A young Asian girl came in.
She was beautiful.
She had nice skin and a happy smile.
I was very glad to see her.
She had on a skimpy pink dress.
She came over to me and ran her hands down my sides.
She gestured for me to follow her because she did not speak English.
She led me into a shower room.
There was a massage table, a large bucket full of water, and a hose.
She gestured for me to lie down on the massage table.
I lay down completely naked.
My nakedness was right there in front of a hot girl.
I liked it very much.
She dumped buckets of warm water on me.
Which felt very good.
Then she got a sponge and covered it in soap.
Then she washed me thoroughly.
My armpits, stomach, feet, cock and asshole.
She cleaned me up real well.
I smiled the whole time.
She kept asking me if I felt nervous.
Prostitutes always say that to me.
After she was done washing me, she poured more hot water on me to get the soap off.
Then she had me stand up.
She dried me off slowly.
I loved it.
Oh, it was nice.
Some assholes would say that I enjoyed it because she was the slave I

bought. But I never told her to do anything or forced any kind of behavior on her.

The female at the Asian Spa was paid to treat me with consideration just for an hour.

I considerately gave her money.

She considerately treated me with respect.

Maybe if everyone was as nice as the Asian Spa females the world wouldn't be such a shitty place.

She led me to a sauna and asked if I would like anything to drink.

I said yes and asked what she had.

She said, "Cola and diet cola."

I said I would take a regular cola.

She got one and left me alone for three minutes.

Didn't know what was going to happen.

Had been told that girls at the Asian Spa have sex with you, but I found it hard to believe anyone during the Information Age.

I fluffed my dick trying to get hard.

Just in case there was sex at the Asian Spa.

She came back and got me, then led me to the same bedroom where my clothes were.

She laid me down on the bed, on my stomach.

She got on my back with her clothes on and started giving me a massage.

It was the best massage of my life.

Started to feel really relaxed.

Really at home.

She made me feel like a person, like all my suffering, all the hell, was worth it.

All the intolerable years of my existence were for something.

That it would be all right.

She flipped me over and massaged the front of my body.

It was so nice.

Almost life-affirming.

She finished the massage and lay down next to me.

I looked at her.

She was so pretty.

She asked what I would like; she gave the prices for a blowjob and a fuck.

I said I would like a fuck.

It was two-hundred fifty dollars.

The price was unimportant; I don't see the difference in the irrationality of spending five hundred on a couch, twenty-five thousand on an SUV, or two-hundred fifty dollars for an hour of pretend love.

She stood up and took her clothes off.

Revealing her soft Asian body.

She lay on the bed.

I crawled on top of her.

We rubbed our nakedness all over each other.

I touched her skin with my hand.

It was so soft and nice.

I kissed her tummy.

Butt.

Legs.

Feet.

Back.

Thighs.

Oh, I kissed and kissed.

There is nothing better than touching and kissing a soft body with nice skin.

She played well with me.

She knew I was sad and alone.

She was probably suffering more because she was thousands of miles away from home.

After ten minutes of kissing and running my hands softly over her body, we had sex.

It was missionary for a while.

And then doggy style for a while.

Then I ate her pussy for a long time.

And then I ate her asshole for a long time.

She had (or maybe faked) an orgasm.

She was probably told to fake at least one orgasm during intercourse because American men enjoy playing that they MAKE or CONSTRUCT the female orgasm. Which is hysterical.

Whether she had a real one or not, it doesn't matter.

I eventually ejaculated.

I came on her ass.

It was so pretty.

My cum lying there on her two little round butt cheeks.

I lay down next to her, smiling.

She placed her small arm over my chest for a few minutes.

She whispered nice sentences to me in the best English she could.

The hour was up and we both put our clothes back on.

I felt miserable that it was over.

She led me to the door.

Before I left though, she gave me a hug.

A gentle hug.

The way hugs should be.

Then she let go, and I left.

I got in my car and was happy.

I felt kind of mad that I had spent two-hundred fifty dollars for one hour of life and didn't get any objects for it.

But in America, you have to spend money to smile.

CRACK WHORE AND CHICKEN STRIPS

I was sitting at Denny's one afternoon.

It was winter and the sun was going down.

So I guess it was around five in the evening.

I was sitting at the counter.

I was reading *About Behaviorism* by Skinner.

Down a couple of seats was this strange woman.

She kept smiling all weird.

And making little disturbances that kept causing me to put my head up.

She was eating chicken tenders and drinking a soda.

She seemed like she was on crack.

Which is common at the Youngstown Denny's.

People of all colors, genders, and ages on crack.

So it was Denny's as usual.

While I was reading I heard in a whisper, "Hey you, come over here."

It was the crazy lady; she wanted me to sit next to her.

I didn't see why not.

She said in a whisper, "Somebody was supposed to pick me up. I don't know where they are. I'm missing a party. I was supposed to dance for these guys. And they were gonna pay me one-hundred fifty dollars. No one has come to pick me up. My dude dropped me off. Yeah, a hundred and fifty dollars, can you fucking believe? I should be at that party. If you pay for my food, I'll give you a blow job."

My first thought was that she is one weird fucking human. Then questions arose.

1. Is she an escaped mental patient?
2. Does she really want me to pay for her food?
3. Would she really give me a blowjob for paying for her food?
4. If I pay for her food, how much of a tip should I leave?
5. Do I want a blowjob from this crazy human?

I said, "Yeah, I'll pay for your food for a blowjob."

She smiled.

I paid for my coffee and her food and left.

We went to the dirty motel down the street.

It was one of those motels where people live, sex is purchased, crack is smoked and spouses are cheated on.

It was perfect for this.

We went into the room.

She immediately took off her clothes and I took off mine.

She began sucking my dick.

But I couldn't focus.

There was something terrifying about this whole event.

There was something terrifying about her.

She was crazy, on crack or something.

Something miserable about her.

Something too miserable.

I couldn't get off.

She offered to put it in her pussy.

But she wasn't wet enough.

I couldn't understand her intentions.

Maybe that was the problem.

She might have been crazy and on crack but she still wanted sex, and that's why she offered it because buying chicken tenders for somebody does not constitute prostitution.

Maybe she was schizophrenic or a feral child.

I lost the need for an orgasm and started thinking about the horror of living.

The horror of living exists for everyone. If anything ties the people of the world together, it is that unceasing horror.

I decided to leave.

Put my clothes on.

Offered her a ride home but she said she would stay in the motel all night.

She asked me if I had a lighter.

I gave her the only one I had.

She lay on the bed with one light on.
She smiled at me.
I smiled back.
Then left.
Got in my car and drove back to Denny's to read *About Behaviorism*.
That was a strange experience.

XXX THEATER

One day I was really bored.
I had the urge to try something new.
Something totally weird.
I heard there was a XXX theater in the Westside of Youngstown.
I had always wanted to go.
So I went.
I drove there.
It was in a shitty neighborhood.
All of Youngstown is shitty.
Youngstown was at its best fifty years ago.
Since then no one has had enough money to build anything new.
There's not even a legitimate grocery store in Youngstown.
Nobody has had money in Youngstown for a long time.
You could tell it had been a real theater at one point.
Where *Citizen Kane* and *Asphalt Jungle* had played.
But there were no more movie theaters in Youngstown.
There was nothing in Youngstown.
I parked the car on the side of the building and got out.
There was a fat man sitting in his car looking around.
I walked past his car and went in.
There was a small porn store in the front.
There was an old woman at the counter.
She was very polite and said, "How you doing today?"
I said, "Fine, how are you?"
She said, "I'm good. Nine dollars for the movie."
I handed her money and went in.
There were men standing at the top of the walkways into the theater.
They were normal-looking men.
They looked like factory workers and schoolteachers.

I assumed they were waiting for someone to come over and offer a blowjob.

I had to go piss so I asked someone where the bathroom was.

He directed me upstairs.

Went up creepy steps to the bathroom.

There was a long hallway that led to a lounge.

There was a couch with an ashtray next to it.

That room led to the bathroom.

I went to the urinal, unzipped and started to piss.

In front of the urinals was a white poster board covered in writing.

"10-09 left side of theater suck your dick."

"I love huge black cock 555-5467."

"I love fat cocks getting hard in my mouth."

"Left side of theater, suck your dick."

"Suck your sick, suck your dick, suck your dick, suck your dick, suck your dick."

I had seen this before at truck stops, so I wasn't surprised.

When I was washing my hands a large black man walked in.

He looked at me and I looked at him.

We had a moment.

I went downstairs.

Sat on the left side of the theater.

Had no idea if that meant anything.

I knew that homosexuals had an intricate system of signs to communicate what they wanted. I could have been sitting in the "Urinate on my face section."

Didn't know. Didn't care.

I watched the movie for a while.

It was an old porn.

There were two males and one female.

The two males took the female's clothes off.

Then one male took the other male's clothes off.

Then that male started sucking the other male's dick.

It was evident to me that I was in a very weird location.

I didn't mind watching the two men suck each other off and fuck.

The female was cute and so was one of the males.

I looked around and saw the big guy from the bathroom sitting five seats away from me.

I looked directly at him for ten seconds and he motioned me over.

He wanted me to suck his dick.

I hadn't sucked a dick in a long time.

But fuck, if you're going to go somewhere weird.

You should be weird too.

I got up, walked over, and sat next to him.

He put his large hand on my thigh.

I'm like five eight and one hundred and ninety pounds. He was like six three and two hundred and fifty pounds.

Was very daunted by his size.

He had an attractive face and I started to get turned on.

He whispered, "Would you like to suck my cock?"

I was like, "All right."

He unzipped his pants and pulled out his cock.

It was fucking huge.

It was six inches long and three inches wide.

And it was still flaccid.

I picked it up, leaned over and put it in my mouth.

It felt nice in my mouth.

All soft and big.

Licked it all over.

Tried to remember things females did that I liked.

I went deep as I could, but I couldn't get very far.

It got harder and harder.

But it never got fully hard.

It would have sucked too much blood out of his brain and caused him to pass out.

I liked sucking his cock in that dark theater.

I liked wrapping my fingers around it, feeling that massive piece of sex in my hand.

I sucked and sucked.

Eventually he blew his load right in my mouth.

It was a massive fucking load.

I thought I was going to vomit.

But I swallowed it down.

Sat up, looked at him and smiled.

He said, "There's some cum on your bottom lip."

I licked it off and said, "Is it gone?"

He said, "Yes."

I sat for a minute staring into the abyss. It didn't look back at me, it just cackled and thought I was funny.

Then the man said, "Take your dick out, I'll suck it."

I did.

He moved his head in the location of my crotch and gave me the best blowjob I ever had.

While he blew me.

I watched the movie.

It was two young lesbians making out and touching butts.

I apologized for not matching him in dick size, but he said, "At least you can stick all of your dick in the hole without worrying. The last time I stuck my dick completely in someone they were in the hospital for two days."

I felt better when he said that.

It still would be cool to have a nine-inch dick.

I blew my load in his mouth.

He sat up.

He swallowed it down.

He put his coat on and said, "Gotta go home. The little woman serves dinner at seven."

He got up and left.

I stood up and walked to the porn store.

While I was there I noticed a room where several people were sitting.

I went in.

There was a Christmas tree with lights.

A television with news on and free coffee.

Four people sitting there.

They all looked ruined.

There was a female crack whore who was forty-five years old. She was wearing a torn-up Browns coat and a short dress.

She looked like hell and a half.

There was a guy sitting by himself wearing fifties-style glasses drinking a cup of coffee, staring into deep space.

The two other males were sitting at a table together drinking coffee, smoking cigarettes and talking.

One was an old guy with a scruffy beard.

The other wore a torn coat and jogging pants.

I poured myself a cup of coffee, sat at a table.

LOVE

In July of 2003, I was about dead.
    Was broke and thousands in debt.
    Had blown whole credit cards on prostitutes and vacations.
    Had school loans and was constantly horny.
    It was open mic night and I needed to get laid.
    I drove to the bar.
    Was alone, like always, alone.
    Other people seemed like aliens to me.
    Other people seemed—
    Distant.
    Unpredictable.
    Weird.
    Contingent.
    Unreliable.
    Untrustworthy.
    Sick.
    Miserable.
    Terrified.
    Dejected.
    Humiliated.
    Incorrigible.
    Malignant.
    Lazy.
    Pathetic.
    Absurd.
    And I also saw all those qualities in myself.
    There are a lot of good reasons to be terrified.
    There is still no excuse for our behavior.
    I got to the door of the bar and waited in line to get my ID checked.
    In front of me was a tall blonde. Her hair was bleached.
    She was taller than me.
    And I found her attractive and unique looking.
    She looked terrified.
    There might be a human in there.
    She got her ID checked and went into the bar.
    I got mine checked and went to the bar and got a drink.
    I sat at the bar for a minute.
    Some zombie came up and sat next to me.

I looked at the zombie and recognized it as my old friend Dustin.

The zombie said, "Hey, you wanna play drums with me tonight? I made up a great song. It's called "Purple Love." Its got a Kinks rhythm mixed with Emo, it's awesome."

I looked straight ahead and said, "Listen Dustin, why do you play that shit? Do you wanna be famous for something?"

"Yeah, of course."

"Well, I'm not going to participate in your bourgeois dream."

"What has happened to you?"

Then the zombie left.

It was about time to go hit on that tall blonde.

She'd had enough time to find a seat, have a drink, and get settled in.

I stood up, looked around and thought, What a bunch of assholes.

Walked to the back room where the stage was.

The tall blonde was there.

I walked straight to her.

Kept getting closer and closer and closer and closer and there I was standing right in front of her.

She was sitting down.

I looked at her and said, "Hey!"

She looked up, saw me, and said, "Yeah!"

I told her my name and then asked, "What's yours?"

"Billy Jean."

That's hot, I thought.

I pulled up a seat and sat next to her.

She was smiling, that was good. Smiles are always positive when flirting.

I asked Billy Jean for her number. She gave it to me and I walked off.

I went to the front of the bar.

Sat down and began to stare again.

I wanted to touch Billy Jean, real bad.

And assumed she'd fuck me.

I ordered another beer and went to the back.

She was sitting in a different location, on a small bench where we could sit together, close, touching, getting all horny and sexy like.

I sat next to her and told her about my dead baby, about trips out west, writing prose, and how I'm a bastard.

She sat there and listened and kept putting her bottom lip in her mouth real sexy like.

I made an inference, she was horny and wanted dick.

And then open mic night was over. We went outside to say goodbye.

She took some steps away from me and I yelled, "Hey!"

Billy Jean turned around.

I grabbed her shirt, pulled her to me and kissed her on the lips.

Then I cackled.

Billy Jean blushed, smiled and walked to her car.

That was the beginning of our sexual life together.

It only got weirder.

Billy Jean was a strange creature.

A combination of Trotsky, de Sade, and Simone de Beauvoir.

But she wasn't any of those three people.

She was Billy Jean.

Fuck yeah!

She was covered in scars from cutting herself with a razor blade when she was going through puberty.

Billy Jean saw the injustice of what America does to females, and how they don't allot females the freedom to even escape it.

She was apprenticed by two secret Marxists from Kentucky.

Coal miner stock that was paid in script.

Billy Jean was playing chess when she was seven.

Billy Jean read trashy romance novels by the age of ten.

Billy Jean grew up poor eating hot dogs and drinking Kool-Aid made with well water.

Billy Jean's house growing up had a coal shoot.

Billy Jean was classy, but you could tell she was still white trash.

And that is what I've always looked for.

Someone like me, white trash but still reads.

We were both very alone.

First there must be a detailed description of Billy Jean's body, so you can properly imagine it.

Billy Jean's Body:

Height: Five feet eleven inches.

Shape: Hourglass.

Arms: Soft twigs.

Hands: Little and cute.

Feet: Also little and cute.

Eyes: Big and green.

Breasts: Perky, almost a C. They cannot hold up a pencil.

Legs: Long and soft.

Skin Tone: A bit darker than white trash blue, even.

Ass: Big, beautiful and round, staring at her ass is the closest I've ever come to feeling transcendent.

One deformity: Her pinky toe. The nail is so small it can barely be seen. It is weird-looking.

*

Here are descriptions of the sex we participated in.

The best sex I've ever had.

One day we were naked sitting on the floor in her living room.

Billy Jean went in the bedroom and came out with some handcuffs.

I looked at her and smiled, "What do we handcuff you to?"

"I don't know, something metal would be good."

We both thought and I said, "How about the leg of the bed?"

"That would be fantastic," said Billy Jean.

We went into the bedroom and I handcuffed her to the bed.

I inserted my dick into her and started pumping.

Then I pulled out and ate her out for a while.

I licked her asshole.

Getting her asshole touched always drove Billy Jean wild.

She had crazy asshole orgasms.

Billy Jean hooted and hollered, screamed bloody murder and came.

I inserted my dick back in her and pumped some more.

Her face was flushed and she looked like she was going to die.

I pulled out.

Crawled on top of her body and jacked off.

I shot my load all over her face.

It almost completely covered her.

Then I stood up and kicked her in the ribs.

She smiled.

I took the handcuffs off and she rubbed the cum all over her face while giggling and smiling.

I realized I had met a strange creature.

A human who enjoyed sex and no longer had any concern for inhibitions.

Billy Jean came to terms with her freedom.

She didn't care about traditions or taboos.

And the ones her parents threw at her, she found silly.

Billy Jean was the antithesis to the American Dream.

I found that all very sexy.

We lived in Youngstown, Ohio too.

It was obvious from the government and economic conditions no one cared how we lived or what we did anyway.

So why should we care about our behavior.

*

One day I was lying on the couch.

I was watching television ladies ice-skating.

Billy Jean came into the room from the kitchen.

She was wearing tight blue jeans and a small black shirt.

She got onto the couch and crawled on her tummy over me.

Placed her ass on my lap.

Billy Jean pushed down her pants and said, "Slap it."

I thought about it a second and decided.

SLAP!

"Again," she said.

SLAP!

She made small noises every time I slapped her bottom.

SLAP!

Five seconds.

SLAP!

Five seconds.

SLAP!

Five seconds.

SLAP!

I did that a long time.

With each slap she made more and more noise.

I got a hard-on.

SLAP!

"Harder," said Billy Jean.

SLAP!

"More at once," said Billy Jean.

SLAP!

SLAP!

SLAP!

Her ass was red and sore.

"Now I want you to do me doggy style over the arm of the couch while hitting me with a belt," Billy Jean said.

"Are you serious?"

"Yes."

She handed me a belt.

It was leather with little holes lined in metal.

Billy Jean took off her clothes and so did I.

She bent over the couch, spread her butt cheeks and I popped my dick in.

I began pumping her.

I held the belt in my hand.

I was not used to engaging in violence.

When my parents hit me it had always been with their fists, never an external object.

So I wasn't sure how to create the effect Billy Jean wanted.

I folded the belt once, held both ends, and started wailing away on her ass and back.

SLAP on her ass!

SLAP on her back!

Still pumping.

SLAP on her ass.

SLAP on her back.

I brutally beat the fuck out of her ass and back.

It was gruesome.

Billy Jean had an orgasm and screamed.

Billy Jean began to cry.

It was real crying, forced out of pain.

It was loud and scary but she wanted more.

I slapped and slapped and slapped her with the belt.

Then I stopped and pulled out and just stood behind her.

Billy Jean hung over the arm of the couch like beef in a slaughterhouse freezer.

I sat down on the floor and looked at her.

She was crying.

She stood up and then lay down on the floor.

Her face had a look of serenity and peace.

It was weird.

She lay like that for ten minutes.

Not talking.

Just lying there still and relaxed.

She eventually came out of it.

Billy Jean said, "Pain is like a drug. It takes you away. It reminds you that you're human, but at the same time makes you an object. No one can tell when you're in pain either, you might be the one hitting me, and I'm making noise. But you don't know if I'm in pain. Physical pain is a secret.

You can only take someone else's word on it. You can't graph or do surveys on physical pain. It is the only thing that is left immeasurable. Physical pain also forces you to recognize that you exist. That you are on a rock, in an indifferent scary universe. And there is nothing metaphysical about that. It is real. When a person screams in pain, the actual pain is only half the noise they make. The other half is the terror at being forced to accept that they exist. All physical pain reminds a person of their own death also, they know even when they get a paper cut that someday some other part of their body is going to get hurt or give out like carburetors or axles do and their body and existence will come to a halting nothingness."

Billy Jean was sexy.

That was for sure.

She looked at me and said, "Slap me in the face."

I didn't know about slapping her in the face. I was afraid I might hurt her.

"Please slap me in the face, hard, so I'll cry. I wanna cry for like fifteen minutes."

She lay on the floor and I got on top of her and inserted my dick.

I began pumping her.

I touched both sides of her face with my hands.

Caressed her cheeks and bit her lips.

Billy Jean closed her eyes.

I picked my right hand off her face and SLAP!

Her whole body shook.

I kept pumping her.

Slowly.

SLAP!

"Harder," she said.

SLAP with the left hand!

"Harder!"

"SLAP!

She opened her mouth and screamed and cried.

She couldn't speak in words anymore.

I could tell she didn't want me to talk.

She wanted to pretend the pain was coming from nowhere.

That the pain was just there.

That it was just put into her.

SLAP!

SLAP!

SLAP!

Tears!
Screams!
Horror!
Fear!
Relentless, unbearable fear!
Screams!
Her whole body shaking!
Convulsing!
Horror!
Tears!
SLAP!
SLAP!
SLAP!
More tears!
Sobbing!
Howling!
Bawling!
SLAP!
SLAP!
SLAP!
Then I got the urge to spit on her face.
I don't know why, maybe she would like it.
Maybe I wanted to play dirty white trash man.
Maybe that is what it was all about, pretending we were normal white trash.
I spit on her face.
She smiled through the tears and screams.
I spit again.
Then SLAP!
I spit.
Her face was soon red and covered with sweat, tears, slobber, and saliva.
I pulled out, crawled on top of her, and blew my load on her face.
Now it was covered with sweat, tears, saliva, and cum.
I lay beside her on the floor.
She rubbed it all together, all over her face.
It was like a Pollock painting of human excrement on her face. All she needed was piss, vomit, and some shit to make it complete.
It was beautiful and would sell for thousands.

*

One night we went to that strip joint I used to go to.

We went in and sat down at the bar.

One dancer's name was Pixie.

She was a beautiful mixed female.

She had a huge round ass and a sweet smile.

Pixie came over to us and sat down.

"Who's this?" Pixie asked.

"This is Billy Jean."

Pixie looked her over and said, "She's cute."

Then Pixie gave Billy Jean a dance.

Billy Jean was wearing a short skirt with little panties.

Pixie pushed the skirt up and rubbed her huge round ass all over Billy Jean's crotch and thighs.

Billy Jean smiled.

Billy Jean liked it.

I liked it too.

I got a hard-on watching.

The dance was over and Pixie found someone else to dance for.

I asked Billy Jean, "So how was it, did you like it?"

She looked at me with a dirty smile and said, "Pixie licked my pussy."

"She licked your pussy? She never licked my dick."

"Yeah, girls get special treatment."

Then another dancer came over. Her name was Candy.

She was into hardcore music and tattoos.

Candy was very rough and almost violent at times.

Her dances were so rough, customers fell off their seats at times.

She came over and sat next to Billy Jean, asked for her name and talked about hardcore music.

Billy Jean liked some hardcore music, so they got along well.

I just sat there and watched.

It seemed that the dancers really liked it when there was a female there.

Billy Jean offered to buy Candy a shot.

Candy accepted.

Billy Jean and Candy were both given shots of whiskey.

They both drank them down.

Then Candy offered to give Billy Jean a dance.

Billy Jean said, "Yes, please." With a sense of urgency.

Candy started the dance.

It was a rough and powerful dance.

Billy Jean's skirt was hiked up to her crotch again.

Then Candy started making out with Billy Jean.

It was violent.

Billy Jean was a very strong and domineering person but Candy took full control of her.

And Billy Jean allowed it.

She was very turned on by females who weren't afraid of sexuality.

I watched and got very hard.

The dance was over and Billy Jean said, "Give me another one."

So Candy danced again for Billy Jean.

Billy Jean knew what was coming so she knew how to behave.

She groped Candy all over, as did Candy with her.

Billy Jean grabbed her butt.

Put Candy's nipples in her mouth.

Ran her hand over Candy's pussy.

Candy took Billy Jean's titties out of her shirt.

Licked them.

Sucked them.

Fondled them.

When the dance ended, I asked for one.

Candy came over to me and rubbed her butt on my crotch.

I groped her butt.

She wrapped her fingers around my dick and jacked me off through my pants.

It was a wild time.

The dances were over and we were out of money.

So we went home.

On the way home Billy Jean said, "I think I would like to work there."

"Are you serious?"

"Fuck yeah. It looks like they have a good time in there. And I can totally make more money there than I can working at the toy store as an asinine cashier."

"Right about that one," I said.

"You think I should?"

"Fuck yeah, sounds like a great occupation for a person with your tastes and boundless sexual energy."

And there it was, an authentic choice by one strange human being named Billy Jean.

*

One boring day Billy Jean and I were lying on the floor naked.

There was nothing to do.

The day looked like it would be unfruitful.

Billy Jean started telling me how her sister urinates during sex on accident.

So I asked her, "Would you urinate on me during sex."

"Yeah, that sounds wonderful."

"Where should we have it? It might stink."

"Upstairs, we never go up there," said Billy Jean.

"All right, go get some towels and I'll meet you upstairs."

She got some towels and I went upstairs.

Billy Jean came up and put the towels on the floor.

She pointed to the floor and said, "Lie down on your back."

I did.

I lay down on my back and she straddled me and inserted my dick.

She pumped and pumped.

I could tell by her face she was trying to piss, but she couldn't.

She eventually gave up and sat on my chest like she was sitting on a toilet.

It took a while, but finally she urinated all over my being.

I loved it, it felt so good.

That warm piss splattering over my chest.

Flowing over my ribs and stomach.

That warm stinky liquid, oh it was nice.

Then she said, "Now you piss on me."

She lay down and I stood above her like I was pissing at a urinal.

I stared down at her for a minute and then began to urinate.

I drank two cans of soda that day and I pissed a lot.

She squirmed as the piss hit her.

It was beautiful like "The Star-Spangled Banner" or "God Bless America."

Billy Jean had a really deep belly button, so a lot of the piss collected there like a small puddle of love, faith, and hope.

I looked down at her urine-covered body and became insanely turned on.

I was also covered in urine.

Got on top of her and fucked her missionary, rubbing our piss-covered chests together.

Oh, it was romantic.

It was like a love scene from a Meg Ryan movie.

It was beautiful.
Rubbing our piss together was powerful.
Illuminating.
Full of grace.
Enlightening.
Scintillating.
Brilliant.
Dazzling.
A festival of cotton.
Billy Jean had an orgasm and then I pulled out and blew my load all over her urine-covered chest.
I knew that I loved her as I looked down at her cum-and-urine-covered chest.
I knew for the first time in my life what love was.
It was a set of behaviors two humans exchanged.
It wasn't a feeling you couldn't control.
There wasn't anything mystical about it.
It was just behaviors.
When two assholes immensely enjoy each other's asshole behavior.
I didn't tell Billy Jean I loved her at that moment though.
I saw no point in it.
Our thoughts were full of dirty sex and human depravity at the moment.
Neither of us needed love or any of that shit to get in the way of a good time.
I wrote a poem about our sweet-like-a-Corvette love after the event.

You urinate on me
I urinate on you
You orgasm
I orgasm
Sometimes you do the dishes
While I cook
Sometimes I do the dishes
While you cook
We eat together
And talk about political theory
It is so nice
When we fuck
You have such a nice pussy

And a big round ass
Oh
Baby
Oh baby

*

One night I was lying on the floor playing video games.

One of those games where you just run around and shoot people.

Those are my favorite.

Well.

Billy Jean came home from work and brought this guy with her.

His name was Nate.

I knew him from the strip joint.

Nicest person.

Very gentlemanly.

Total cokehead and drunk.

But still a great person.

I knew what was going to happen next.

Billy Jean wanted to have sex with him.

I had no problem with that.

But I really didn't feel like watching.

I had already gotten off that night to some pics on the computer.

I knew Nate was sad, miserable, and heartbroken.

He had just gotten over a divorce and worked fifty hours a week as a construction worker.

So his life wasn't easy.

I went to the bedroom and read a book about Youngstown.

I heard them flirt out there and heard the noises of sweet sad sex.

I had to go to the bathroom and had to walk through the living room and saw them.

Nate was on top of her slowly fucking her.

He was imagining romance and love.

I had been there before and still was a lot of times when I had sex with Billy Jean.

I stood there for a while just looking.

As I watched them have sex I realized that depraved sex is just one of the activities we do to escape this shit-pool of lies and cheap labor.

Tah Dah.

CIVILIZATION

A man or woman way back in the day.

Stood next to the Euphrates.

Looking at the water.

Thinking, because there was a problem.

There was a food shortage.

The tribe was going to die.

The person stood and thought for hours.

It was a hot day in spring.

The person looked around and noticed and realized that where they shit, the plants they liked to eat grew strangely all in one place.

The person started digging around in the shit and saw that the plants were popping out of the little round pieces of shit.

So the person grabbed a bunch of seeds and ran back to the tribe and yelled, "Look, these are what make our food, these things."

They stared at him like an asshole.

"No, I'm serious. These little things go in the ground, and then our food comes up after the cold part of the year."

A person of the tribe said, "Shut the fuck up! Are you stupid, the Turtle God Dingy Baka makes the food grow after we pee in the holy puddle."

"No, I really think these little things make our food grow."

"Whatever, you plant those stupid little things on your own fucking time. But if it makes Dingy Baka mad, we are going to kill you. You got that motherfucker!"

"All right, all right."

So the person planted a bunch of the same little things that were near the plants the tribe ate in a single area.

Soon food starting growing.

Eventually they figured out that water helped the plants grow and then later, how to harness animals to help them grow food more efficiently.

*

After many generations.

One man had much more fertile land than the others.

He went to the tribe and said, "I cannot work all my land by myself. I need help, are there any men who have shitty plots that want to leave them and help me work my land?"

Several men said, "Yes, our land is shitty. We will come and work for you."

The one man with the bountiful piece of land became very powerful, and took control over the tribe.

*

After several generations a man who also had bountiful land went to the tribe and said, "That land that I work is mine, and I want it to go to my son. But I want to ensure it is my son. How do I do that?"

The men talked for several days and concluded, "Pick a woman, and don't let her leave the house no matter what."

And that's what the man did.

He walked amongst the tribal women and chose one.

The father of the woman said, "You can't just take my daughter, she cooks and makes clothes."

So the rich man gave some money to the father and took his daughter to his home.

The woman did not understand it.

Women had always been equal with men.

Everyone had always enjoyed the freedom of sex.

But, "Those days are over. We have to worry about our property now," the man said to the woman.

Eventually cities were built.

Taxes were invented.

And civilization blossomed.

*

Sometimes I get a knife.

And cut little slits in my skin.
Blood drips out.
I rub my finger in it.
Prostitutes always get their eyes cut out.

*

The President came to Youngstown.
He brought the military with him.
The President had the military round up all the ghetto trash, Latinos, and poor white trash.
The military told the people the President was going to give them a present.
So the people happily went.
Thousands stood before the stage waiting for their present.
The President came out and said, "I am tired of you people living here.
"You make America look bad.
"You're always drunk.
"You're always fighting.
"A lot of you have taken to Oxy, weed, heroin, Valium, and a good amount crack.
"There are no jobs for you here. Can you not see that?
"Most of the people of Youngstown have left, the smart ones.
"But you have stayed, hoping for a better day.
"Even though you are completely conscious that such a day will never come.
"I'm going to do you all a favor.
"I'm using the Great American Military to relocate you to another area.
"You will be happy where you're going. I send people there all the time and they never complain again."
The crowd screamed and hollered.
But The President did not care.
He just walked off the stage like nothing happened.
He didn't even look at the people.
So the people started walking home to get their stuff and get in their cars.
But the military men said, "Stop, you aren't going anywhere, you pieces of shit have to walk."
The trash of Youngstown screamed, "We need our shit to move!"
So the military shot some Youngstown trash.

The people started moving then.

Nobody knew where they were going.

Most were too drunk or high to care.

As they were leaving they could see bulldozers come into town, getting ready to knock over buildings.

They walked for several days.

Some were fed, some were not.

One would think the people of Youngstown would have put up a fight.

But they believed wholeheartedly that The President would lead them somewhere beautiful, like Florida or California.

Weeks passed and it didn't seem like they were going anywhere.

They figured out they were moving west, but where they did not know.

Around the fourth week, the military stopped feeding them.

They became delirious.

There were no more drugs or booze to be found.

Sometimes they would pass through a town and people would look at them and laugh.

Eventually they were led to a giant hole in the ground.

But they were so tired and hungry by then they didn't even notice. And walked peacefully into the hole.

Over a hundred thousand humans were in that hole.

They all sat down.

The blacks were down in the hole with their weaves and cornrows.

The poor whites were down there with their mullets and Tweety Bird shirts.

Together at last.

The hole was lined with military men.

Holding machine guns.

The men stared down at the Youngstown trash and fired.

Screams were heard.

Grenades were thrown in the hole.

Body parts flew everywhere.

The Youngstown trash could hear the military men laughing while they shot and threw grenades.

It took several hours but eventually everyone in the hole was either dead or badly wounded to the point of being unable to walk.

The military men stopped firing.

They sat on the edge of the hole smoking and drinking booze, picking off the remaining Youngstown trash one by one for target practice.

After about two days.

None were left.

Bulldozers came.

Perhaps the same ones that knocked down the city of Youngstown, pushed dirt over its citizens.

*

Two old white men wearing expensive suits were sitting in an office in Youngstown. One's name was Bob, the other was Tony.

The year was 1876.

Tony said to Bob, "If we send some boats to Southern Europe and get some Italians and Greeks to work for us, we can pay them less than the Germans and British we have working for us now."

*

The Code of Hammurabi: Written around 1740 B.C.E.

Eye for an Eye, laws to protect private property.

Written language exists to protect private property.

The Nile River: Egypt: 2050 to 1652 B.C.E.

The Pharaoh: The God King: At least the rulers didn't lie about what they thought they were back then.

They used stone dishes. That must've sucked.

The Assyrians: 700 B.C.E. They kicked ass and took names later.

They won because they could create terror.

Harappan Culture: A peaceful culture: 3000 to 1800 B.C.E.

This brilliant culture thrived for 1300 years. And then it disappeared. None of it was left when the Aryans arrived.

Krishna says stupid shit: 200 B.C.E.

Krishna tells poor people to die for the rich because it is their duty, because rich people are gods.

Reincarnation: Created by Aryans: Outside invaders to India: Between 1500 and 1000 B.C.E.

A stroke of genius by the rich to keep poor people stupid and retarded.

Greeks: 750 to 500 B.C.E.: A lot of shit written down.

People were naked a lot, some good philosophy, some good plays, homosexuality. If you were a woman or a slave, your life sucked.

The Roman Empire: Founded by Romulus and Remus 753 B.C.E. The shit ends 500 C.E. So for 1,253 years Rome thrived.

Wars, sex, and random insanity by their rulers.

Christianity: Gospels written between 50 and 150: Loser fan club.

No evidence of Jesus' existence, a lot of wasted lives and dead people because of it.

Mayan Culture: 300 to 850: A really cool calendar.

Makes written language to record lives of rich people.

The Rise of Islam: 600s: Cruel stupidity.

Another stroke of genius by the rich, Islam told poor people they would go to heaven if they die for the economic interests of the rich. Some inventions here and there.

Islam still reigns in the middle east, meaning the people still hate themselves.

*

Looking back over history.

A lot of shit went down for a long time.

Harappan culture for over a thousand years. All those people working to keep that culture going.

All those hands that built and created that culture.

I look at the pictures of the ruins and imagine the millions of people who walked the streets of their cities.

The gossip they spoke, what they did in their spare time.

For over a thousand years humans living under the Harappan flag.

3,800 years before I even existed, their culture was gone.

All the people of the great Harappan culture dead before I even came into existence.

All the humans that have existed since then did not know one human from that culture.

All that history.

The history books say the decline and eventual disappearance of the Harappan culture is a mystery.

There is no mystery here in America.

The reasons can be seen on every TV channel.

Written on everybody's face.

The people have given up.

They are too mentally deranged to even revolt.

They have to take drugs and drink booze to quiet all the American thoughts.

*

On a carrier in the Persian Gulf.

A man sits deep in the ship.

At 8pm it is his job to push a button to send missiles to an Iraqi village.

He sits there thinking, I hope I get sent to the Philippines soon. I would love to stick my dick into one of those nice little Philippine girls soon.

While he sits there he is eating a bag of chips.

Over his headset he gets the order.

He puts down his bag of chips.

Pushes the button.

Then thinks, I would really love some pussy right now.

*

An Arab man is sitting in his kitchen, sweating, eating a bag of chips.

He's dead now.

*

Let's get personal.

I am one human among six and a half billion.

Like if you had six and a half billion pieces of Pez, and you took out one piece and sat it next to the giant pile.

I would be that one piece.

I am one piece of Pez.

Yes I am.

I live on Earth, in America. Red, white, and blue MO FO!

Inside the state of Ohio.

In a city named Youngstown.

I live in a house.

Remember this all comes from my heart.

You know?

The other day my shit was so hard and big, I had to cut it in half with a coat hanger to get it down the toilet.

I think my ex-fiancée was an intersex baby.

The only time I smile is when I'm thinking about sex.

When I get drunk and I'm home alone, I download free scat porn.

I like to watch four huge black men pound the shit out of one tiny white girl.

I like calamari. That's squid.

It turns me on when my girlfriend fucks other men.

I like it so much; I have her tell me about it.

I think *Gone with the Wind* sucks.

My boxers always have skid marks.

I beat children.

I once spent a year lodged in your mother's asshole.

When I was in high school I punched a girl.

I killed forty-five babies and a water buffalo during the Vietnam War.

I drink a lot of bottled water.

Sometimes I think dirty thoughts about men, mostly sucking their dick. I got hemorrhoids, can't take it up the ass. I would bleed like a stuck pig.

I got a broken-down car in my driveway.

I eat meat.

I like guns.

I eat candy.

When I'm depressed I eat ribs or go to the Asian buffet.

I rarely ever eat pussy.

I can go hours without cumming because of these anti-depressants I was on for six years straight. Momma aren't you proud?

I have no interest in getting anally raped by a donkey, just like I have no interest in having children or getting married.

I do enjoy watching women suck horse cock though.

I view my existence as pointless. So what?

I view your existence as pointless, bitch! So let's fuck and have a good time.

I get drunk almost every day. Those are the good days.

I don't vote. Voting is for rich people.

Don't have cable.

Don't have money.

Don't have an SUV.

Oh, I forgot one thing. I might be going bald.

Also, I had scabies.

*

Voice of the Republican Party: "We are correct, we are correct, we are correct, we are Gods, we make you suffer for your own good. We don't kill our own ethnicity, we kill other ones."

Voice of the Democratic Party: "Don't smoke, drink, go to strip joints, and don't ever fucking eat candy. We are pointless."

Voice of the Moderates: "We are pussies who wait to see who is gonna win."

Voice of the Green Party: "We are a bunch of upper-middle-class assholes who listen to Bob Dylan, stopped maturing the day of the Kent State shootings, and don't know shit about Middle America."

The Voice of the Communist Party: "We are correct, we are correct, we are correct, but we kill our own people, not others."

*

Humans aren't hard to figure out. The problem is, you have to admit you are one of them to do so.

*

This book is my asshole.
My books are not my babies.
They are my assholes.
After this book gets published.
I will have three assholes.

*

I'm sitting in a crappy house that hasn't been remodeled since the sixties.
There are holes in the walls.
I'm sitting on a thrift store couch.
Naked.
Smoking cheap cigarettes.
My girlfriend whose name is Fuck Supreme told me today why see-through thongs have cotton over the pussy.
I asked her, "Why is there cotton there?"
She responded, "Because the soft fabric makes the female aroused all day, she is wet for so long that she gets a yeast infection."
"Wow," I said.

*

Things you should know before you die.
There is a worldwide gay organist subculture.

Women started the French and Russian revolutions.

Your mother doesn't love you.

Violence helps.

The meaning of life is that each human is striving to one-up one of his or her parents and at the same time trying to piss off the other one. People usually choose which one matters most to them and strive harder for that one.

*

There is a man.

Sitting in a white trash bar.

He is by himself.

It is Friday night.

There are a lot of people there.

Stevie Ray is playing on the jukebox.

The man speaks to no one.

He has no friends there.

He doesn't want any friends there.

If he knew people there.

He would have to talk.

And what he wants least is to talk.

He likes to hear people talk.

He listens to the other people's conversations.

About football, drugs, strip joints, work, etc.

He likes to hear people talk.

But he doesn't want to have the responsibility of responding back.

He doesn't want to think of funny shit to say.

Of opinions on anything.

He is tired of opinions.

They go nowhere and do nothing.

Like most Americans, he prefers action.

He has read philosophy and much literature.

He knows the phrases, the big words, the names, and ideas to have to give opinions.

But it doesn't interest him.

Nothing much interests him anymore.

He just drinks.

And waits.

For what, he doesn't know.

But he waits.
Sometimes he doesn't wait.
Sometimes he just kind of exists like the ashtray or the shot glass.
Those moments are his favorite.
When he isn't thinking.
When he just exists.
The man doesn't have much.
He has no job, which means he has no money.
His girlfriend buys his smokes and food.
And that is all he gets.
She doesn't have much to spare.
She's gotta pay the bills.
He understands that.
The man wants a job.
But he's got no education.
No skills, nothing.
He and his girlfriend only have one car.
So that makes it tough because she has to be at work and school at certain times.
He knows any job he gets won't pay much.
Maybe six dollars an hour.
But he'll take what he can get.
The gun is to his head.
Inflation has raised the price of gas, food, water, heat, and cigarettes.
The man keeps drinking, and listening to people talk.
The man doesn't have many options.
His credit is ruined and he's got no skills.
He would like to start over.
Go back to the age of nineteen and try it all over again.
But he's twenty-four and too many years have passed.
Only five.
But five is enough to destroy a man's possibilities and hope in the world.
Now the man drinks alone.
Sipping his drink, waiting for this era of stupidity to end.
But the man sees no end in sight.
So he keeps ordering drinks.
Getting drunker.
Trying to make himself as stupid as the era he lives in.
The other people in the bar are like him.
Hopeless, forsaken, without a reason.

They keep going, so he keeps going too.
The gun is at the man's head.
The gun is always there.
The son of a butcher and a factory worker.
In a country that lives by the gun.
In a lawless city.
The gun, he thinks.
The gun.
I have to take six dollars an hour, maybe just minimum wage.
Because of the gun.
He sees the gun at that moment pointed at everyone's heads.
They all know the guns are there.
Telling silly lies about the gun.
The gun is written in the stars.

The saddest thing, thinks the man, is that the gun is held by all of us. By the people who love me. And at the moment of my birth, a man came and pointed the gun right at my head.

So the man drinks to forget about the gun.

*

Ever think about killing yourself?

I mean just to get it over with.

Like how people say, "I got a cavity. I have to go to the dentist. I might as well go tomorrow *to get it over with.*"

Like that.

Are you ever sitting there alone in your home eating dinner by yourself and think thoughts similar to these:

I should kill myself.

Death sounds fucking horrible.

I really want it to be over and done with.

First, nothing happens after.

Second, everyone is going to judge you after you're dead.

And third, you have to die in a certain way, car wreck, gunshot, cancer, something horrible.

And for sure if you live long enough you will die toothless, shitting yourself.

*

My mother said, "Goo goo gaa gaa."

The pundit said, "Goo goo gaa gaa."

Then the hammer came down saying, "Diddle diddle, eat your sandwich, scum fucker!"

And I knew the truth then—metaphysical and dumb.

Today I applied for a job.

Perhaps they will hire me.

Then I work for the goo goo and the gaa gaa.

Drink the pussy juice.

Licking sweat off a stripper's tit in July.

Cost me ten dollars.

Now the guns fire.

The band plays. They get mowed down by long-range missiles and blogs.

"More drugs," she yelled.

"My father is a metallurgist," she said while sniffing a line.

Poor heroin addicts aren't interesting. The news will not run a story on a trailer park girl shooting up in a whore house in downtown Youngstown.

Mother of three, suburbia, sniffing crystal meth, give her a reality television show.

Are you engaged yet?

Have I raped you!

School teachers in chorus: "Goo goo gaa gaa, goo goo gaa gaa!"

The crackhead: "I put my guitar in F sharp, then they shall know my awesome power."

Yes, yes, yes, yes.

Last year I spent over $42,000 on suffering.

Why can't I make them suffer? Voice of narcissist.

Shoot the cows full of estrogen, make the nine-year-old girls horny, make the boys not get horny till they are fifteen, then they tea bag, suck nuts, and smoke weed to make it worse.

America is the greatest country on the planet.

18,000 dead a year because of no health insurance.

Have three jobs, still not full-time.

Her twat bled, thank god, not pregnant.

Have baby, no money, but persist!

We march to the hospital in droves. We stare at babies. We take pictures of the babies. Then we are beaten and sent to prison.

The Bastille has returned.

Dregs butt-fucked, sucking cock, getting tattoos, learning hell, shank you with a tooth brush.

Turn on the Food Channel, kill the time kill the time kill the time kill the time kill the time kill the time kill the time focus on food it's simple easy explainable!

Don't examine the core.

The inner relations.

Don't put things in context, shoot them dead!

Give the *Time/Newsweek* lobotomy!

Get drunk, ramble about how you care!

Don't go to the laundry mat and goo goo while fingering yourself.

Sniff that coke, take that Oxy, throw down those pills. You've had a hard day at work, you deserve it.

Homeless crackhead: "I'm starving."

Me: "I know you're fucking starving, but I gotta get drunk with ten dollars."

Get your dick sucked in a van for fifty dollars.

Prostitutes are independent contractors.

Factory workers are temp workers.

Three months, goodbye motherfucker, no health insurance or raise for you!

Go to this factory, pick up boxes, go fast or be fired, seven dollars an hour.

Examine rubber parts under magnifying glass for $6.50 an hour.

Too slow, fired!

Broke leg when twenty years old, cost forty thousand dollars, can't pay back, no health insurance, ruined life.

Hit somebody with car, broke their leg, then sued, Denny's cook, lost case, owe $500,000, life ruined.

The hammer comes down!

On my head, blood, brains, and genius scattered on floor.

Watch television, hear gunshots from porch.

Cameras in the projects.

Watching the movements.

At Denny's, five in the morning, woman screaming: "My man just got shot. My man just got shot. Give me a cheeseburger."

All this while government argues over Ten Commandments in court-house in the south.

Shoes with holes.

Blistered fingers.

THE COLLECTED WORKS VOL. I

Bruised eyes.

The knees of a whore scarred from pavement.

The drug dealer shoots a man!

No laws here.

On television they argue in suits.

With nicely combed hair.

The pundits and politicians scream at each other, "Goo goo gaa gaa, goo goo gaa gaa!"

We listen hoping that someday they will mention humans, or at least speak with sentences that correspond with reality.

No we go on, we drink, fight, fuck.

Not a solution, but it will do for now.

Not enough accurate information.

All blogs, all sitcoms, all goo goo gaa gaa newspaper articles with flashy headlines.

Top stories:

Penguins fuck in movie theaters.

Famous actor cheats on wife even though he is actually gay.

Terrorist found putting mustard bombs in ham sandwiches.

Stripper warfare down on Market Street.

Breed the chickens, shoot them full of toxins, kill them, and serve them at the local fast food restaurant.

*

A man and woman are in their living room.

They have been dating for two years.

Had sex a million times, had a million laughs together, know each other's dirty little secrets.

A usual relationship.

*

I saw regular people ruined by Youngstown, coked-up, pregnant, and imprisoned.

Who sat in her small living room sniffing coke nine months pregnant still dancing watching NBC because it was the only channel that came in clearly.

Who had seven miscarriages, two babies taken away, stoned, and will die by thirty because of a blood clot in her lungs because of being thrown through a window.

Who sold crack, shot a man, and went to prison.

Who sold coke, shot a man, and went to prison.

Who had sex with an asshole, got accused of rape by her mother, took a personality test, scored badly, and sent to prison for five years.

Who grew up with me, went to the Marines, became schizophrenic, and is now a crackhead.

Who I loved, gained weight, had a baby, and married out of tradition.

Who spent years in the mental ward, barely graduated, married, got stoned, sucked lawyer dick for money, and gave birth to a child they hate.

Who rose up from poverty to be a slumlord and bar owner, sniffed coke, married four times, and is drinking herself to death.

Who worshipped cowboys and moonshiners, who got stoned, graduated college, ran drugs, and now under ground.

Who grew up getting beat, is gay, who claimed bankruptcy, and has worked at the same factory for five years.

Who drank himself stupid, thought people liked him, hates the world, plays video games till sleeping, and won't leave his house.

Who is four eleven, female, and drinks a fifth of V.O. every night.

Who rides his bike asking for three dollars to get one more rock to get through the day.

Who grew up eating hot dogs, watching her dad go from factory job to another, and now subdues her mind with dirty sex.

Who flunked out of college, who owes twenty thousand in bills, and can barely speak.

*

A man and woman are eating together.

Chinese takeout.

They sit across from each other at the kitchen table.

The woman talks and talks and talks.

Nothing she says matters.

The man has dated women who were quiet and spoke of things that mattered.

He misses those women.

But she is what he could find.

The woman talks: I had to do this, and she said that, and I was like betrayed, you know, and I'm trying so hard, but it never comes out right, because so and so, and I did this really well, did you see this movie, it was great, blah blah blah death.

The man responds with simple yes or no answers.

She doesn't care.

The man stares at her and thinks while she blah blahs: Why doesn't she take her clothes off, I'm only here because I want to fuck her, she doesn't even ask me what my last name is, it is just blah blah blah, she can blah blah naked, I would let her talk her stupid head off while penetrating her, well, at least it is killing time. It is not like I have anything else to do.

So the man sat and she talked, and that was that.

*

This is how you get a shitty job.

For males:

Before your interview, don't shave. Also, wear jeans.

Look like you really need money, like you need money so bad you can't even afford a razor.

For females:

Make sure and notify them that you have a baby. If you don't have a baby, wear shitty clothes.

And make sure to use the phrase, "I really need money."

*

I like to get drunk.

And listen to folk blues men like Robert Johnson, Big Bill Broonzy, and Lead Belly.

When I'm drunk listening to them.

I don't feel alone.

They didn't have no money either.

They were assholes too. They drank, smoked, and had good times in bars.

They didn't have it easy either.

None of them made any money playing their music.

They had to work shitty jobs to pay the bills.

They didn't have much of nothing but random compliments they would get on how their music cheered some poor bastard up.

They understood what music and art was created for and why people enjoy it.

People come home from work or are listening to the radio at work and the song takes them away, a human goes into the song and escapes but at the same time, the escape is that they don't feel so alienated and alone.

They are escaping their alienation by realizing that there are other people out there, with the same problems as them, the same hardships.

It gives one a sense of unity.

*

Reality television show idea: Take a billionaire. Stick him in the projects with no money and have him live there for a year.

Contests:

Crack smoking.

How many forties can he drink in one night.

His brother gets shot and his boss won't let him take a day off work the next day.

He gets shot in the leg and has to crawl to the hospital.

And 50 Cent hosts.

Another show idea: *The Ultimate Survivor*.

Take an American liberal who is getting their masters at a private school. And drop him off in Porte Prince, Haiti.

Contests:

He gets $100 bills stapled to him and then placed in the middle of a busy street.

He has to kill a cat and eat it.

He gets sold to a rich Haitian as a boy toy for two weeks.

Then he has to make a raft and sail to America.

And hosted by Wyclef Jean.

*

Were you ever drinking one night and thought, I would like to kill myself, but I just don't have a good reason. I wish my daughter would get hit by a car or I was a ground troop in Iraq so people would say after I did it, "He had his reasons."

*

Make it all go away!

Please!

Make it all go away!

*

The other night I was delivering a pizza to a hospital.

I had to deliver two pizzas while I was there.

I went into the building.

A nurse came over and paid for her pizza and gave me a four-dollar tip.

A doctor came over next and paid for his pizza and gave me a three-dollar tip.

America.

*

The only difference between children and adults is that adults pay bills.

*

What terrifies me.

The majority is, has, and will be mediocre.

They do what the others say is good.

Which implies most human lives are pointless.

The terror lies in how they deal with their pointlessness.

*

I want to have some kids.

So I can beat the shit out of them.

*

There are a lot of long nights here in Youngstown.

When the sun doesn't wanna come up.

You just sit on your couch, staring at your living room.

Looking at what little you have.

Your fourteen-inch television without cable.

Most of the time only NBC works.

Your used couches.

Your used coffee table.

Trying to think of something to do.

Some activity that will make you happy.

That will make it worth living.
Most of the time there is no activity affordable.
So you sit there.
Staring.
Trying not to think.
Trying not to notice how there you are.
Just there, surrounded by your junk.
Junky objects and junky people.
You go to a bar and get drunk sometimes.
Come home and sleep.
Sometimes you're lying there on a day off wishing you had to go to work, because work will give you something to think about that isn't you.
The night goes on.
And you eventually fall asleep.
And have strange dreams about how you can move things with your mind.
You call someone on the phone sometimes, trying to have a little conversation.
And they tell you about how they just got a DUI.
Or they are pregnant and don't want the baby.
Basically always something horrible.
Sometimes you don't call.
You surf the internet looking for a porn picture to jerk off to.
Or write a five-page letter to your dude in the pen.
Sometimes you put in a movie.
And watch it.
But the people in it are always more attractive and richer than you, so it just makes you depressed.
And other times you decide to break things.
But if you break something you have to clean it up.
Most of the time you do nothing.
You just wait to be so tired you fall asleep.

*

I try to make friends.
But I never can.
I can't handle people.
They never stop lying.
I can't think anymore.

Burning Babies

DEATH OF AN OUTLAW

"I'm going to kill myself," said Josey into a cell phone in Kentucky.

"Oh, don't do that. You'll go to hell," said his mother from her house in Youngstown.

"I'm serious you fucking assholes!"

Josey was in a poorly painted gray van that was once red.

He had to paint the van gray because THEY were coming, he said.

Josey was convinced people were coming for him.

Josey was right.

Two days earlier THEY found him.

Beat the fuck out of him, busted up his genitals, and left him for dead.

He crawled to the hospital and stayed there for two days.

That was somewhere in Georgia.

Now he was driving his van down the Kentucky highway to Ohio, to Youngstown, his home, where he'd matured into an unhealthy fucked-up adult.

The conversation continued.

"Josey, you can't kill yourself, I love you."

"I can't take it anymore! I'm serious, I can't fucking take it."

They randomly spoke like this as he drove home.

Josey screamed in the van, pounded his fists on the steeling wheel, punched himself in the face, wringing his hands, growling, making fists, crying, bawling, screaming, wailing!

He screamed, "Fuck you all, who am I! Fuck fuck fuck! WHY! WHY! WHY! How did this happen! Can't someone make this stop! Can't someone help me! Fuck fuck fuck!"

He drove for hours and hours like that.

Going home to where he grew up, to parents who never cared about him.

Going home to a place where no one cares about anyone.

There is no time to care, work must be done.

And when the time-clock is punched, errands like going to the bank, writing out bills, sending boxes, buying toothpaste, eating ice cream, checking your credit report, going to the dentist, back doctor, psychic, and Asian Spa must be done.

Shit must be done; there is no time for friendship, no time for sex, romance, conversations, swimming, relaxation, no time for happiness. Work must be done!

Josey had done his work.

It gave no rewards.

Josey graduated high school with good grades. No scholarship, no money, no sex for that.

Josey graduated from a state university with a business degree because his parents said he should go.

No rewards for that.

What does the world of free-market Information Age business want with a kid who has a business degree from a state university, nothing, jack shit, no rewards there, no sex, no big house in Burbank, no 1970 mint-condition Camero, nothing but wasted time and money.

So there was Josey: a thirty-year-old man wearing dirty underwear, jeans with holes in them, a mullet, and shirt with beer and coffee stains on it driving a shitty fucked-up van down a shitty highway to his shitty home where no one cared he existed.

Josey continued to scream and holler at the top of his lungs while running the thoughts through his head.

Should I kill myself!

Should I not kill myself!

Josey didn't recite Hamlet's speech in his head, but it resembled it. Hamlet's speech is in no way special; it is what all humans who kill themselves say in their heads while deciding to pop a cap in their face.

Josey didn't know Hamlet's speech either.

He went to college but didn't know shit about literature, painting, or classical music.

He didn't care, why should he?

A lot of people have read Hamlet and continued to kill themselves.

People committing suicide always make some kind of fantastic wager like if there is a shooting star in the next five minutes I won't hang myself from this tree, or if the wind blows east I won't do it.

I assume Josey thought of a similar concept.

He was probably like, "If the next car is blue, I won't kill myself."

Well, the next car that passed was blue, but he still wanted to kill himself.

He screamed in horror!
Bitched!
Smacked the dashboard!
Punched his own face!
Moaned!
Screamed!
But there was no answer.
Josey was out there alone.
Alienated disfigured!
Alone!
Full of violence!
Other people seemed like aliens, non-humans, beasts.
He pulled the van over to the side of the highway.
He picked up his shotgun, loaded one bullet, and stepped out of the van.
Went over to the side of the van.
Put the gun in his mouth.
What are the very last thoughts of a person who actually kills themselves, who actually does it knowing there is no escape from the choice they have made. I don't know.
I'm not going to assume that I know either. I'm not an asshole.
Well, he had the end of the gun in his mouth.
And BLAST!
Nothing happened, Josey died, that was all.
A huge hole was in the back of Josey's head.
Josey no longer moved.
His heart stopped.
His thoughts stopped.
Nothing remained of Josey.
No more fun for Josey.
No more dancing.
Sex.
Drinking.
Partying.
Good times.
Goals.
Self-help quotes.
Movies.
Hunting.
Golf.

Music.
Work.
Tying his shoes.
Putting on his shirt.
Taking showers.
Swimming.
Conversations.
Needing to impress anyone.
Caring what other people think about him.
Needing to sell his labor to cheap no-good assholes.
Assholes.
Family.
Need to hope.
Lottery tickets.
Police.
Prostitutes.
Saying cheese when taking pictures.
Christmas.
Easter.
Fourth of July.
U.S. Presidents.
Religions.
Computers.
Prime-time sitcoms.
No more.
No more.
No more.
Josey died, and the world went on without him.
I don't know if he has a tombstone. I've never been to his grave.
Perhaps it is unmarked.
It should be.
It should say:
Here Lies an Outlaw.
Because that is what he was in his last years: an outlaw.
I think he was a drug runner for the Mexicans.
Don't know though, but that's everybody's guess.

His heroes were from the movies like all good American kids. A lot of outlaws; moonshiners were his favorite. Being a moonshiner wasn't in big demand when he became an outlaw, but drugs were, and that's what he did.

*

My mother always said to me, "Monco, when starting a book, always start with a suicide, a murder, or a rape."

So, I started the book with suicide; it's her own son's, so I hope she's not mad. But since I had the chance of impressing her by using her advice I did it anyway.

I hope she is very happy with this first chapter.

A NERVOUS MAN

My girlfriend and I were eating dinner. Her name is Delphine. She is pretty, nice clear skin, long legs, big ass, and giant green eyes.

The dinner was Mexican Hamburger Helper. We put taco cheese and chips in it to make it better. Otherwise it is practically inedible.

Delphine: "I saw Jeff today at school."

Monco: "What'd he say?"

Delphine: "He said he couldn't come out with us anymore because his counselor said he needed to relax. So he has to do twenty minutes of exercise before going to sleep."

Monco: "Is that so?"

Delphine: "He also said he was going to sit in his room for three weeks and take pictures of random objects with perfect lighting. Then he burped, and it smelled like balogna death, and he left."

A BLOODY NEW YEAR'S

I think it was New Year's. It must have been.

Well, I went to the bathroom. First I must tell you at Christmas this kid named Vito came over and cooked the thickest goddamned alfredo I've ever eaten. It almost killed me it was so thick. Best alfredo I've ever eaten, though.

Well, I ate the shit.

And because I was drinking I forgot to take a lactaid.

When I consume any milk products, I get constipated.

It sucks.

I forgot to take the pill and I had a death-of-god shit the next day. It almost killed me.

I pushed and pushed and pushed and only a little turd came out.

For the next several days the same experience, pushing and pushing and pushing only to squirt out one little meaningless bullshit turd.

That day I was on the toilet for over two hours.

No luck.

Just pain.

The shit was compacted in my stomach and it hurt like hell.

I didn't know what the hell was wrong with me.

I got up from the toilet, put on my jeans, sweater, and jacket, tied my shoes, got the car keys and drove down the street to a Rite Aid.

I walked to the pills section.

Started reading the boxes of some of the pills I took during that week.

Looked at the back of the Advil box; it said that if you take more than six Advils a day your stomach will bleed.

I took like twenty a day that week. That caused a minor panic.

The question arose: is my shit covered with dry blood and that's why I can't shit?

Didn't think that was the reason though.

Went to the hemorrhoid medication section.

Read the back of those boxes. One of them said it relieves constipation.

"This must be it!" I said out loud to myself.

"My hemorrhoids are causing my constipation. That's awesome!" I also said that out loud.

So I bought a tube of Preparation H and some ass-wipes.

Went to the counter and gave the clerk a big smile of pride because I had figured out why I couldn't shit.

Drove home.

Inside, Delphine was sleeping on the living room floor.

We have to sleep in the living room because the windows in the bedroom are so drafty we both get sinus headaches and are congested.

I woke her up.

She looked at me like I was an asshole.

But I was very excited. I said, "Delphine, I figured out why I can't shit. It's my hemorrhoids."

She looked at me with joy in her eyes.

Delphine and I went to the bathroom.

I took the tube of Preparation H out of the box. It had a thin two-inch nozzle on it. I asked her to insert it into my ass and then squeeze the bottle.

I took my pants and boxers off and bent over.

Held the toilet while she sat on the floor.

Told her, "Delphine, squirt some out and mush it around my asshole for awhile, then kind of open my asshole with your finger, and then slowly stick it in."

Delphine put some on her middle finger. She smeared it around.

Then kind of eased her middle finger about half an inch in.

Pushed the tube up my anus and squeezed.

Delphine let it sit in my asshole for a little bit, then took it out.

But something unexpected happened. I got really hard and horny.

I looked back at her and said, "Delphine, I'm really horny now."

She was like, "Oh, yeah, whatcha gonna do about it?"

"Penetrate your vagina."

And we went to the living room to have our first sex of the year 2005.

3 DOLLARS

There's this middle-aged black guy.

Who looks like shit.

Who wears a baseball cap down low almost over his eyes.

He is always on Belmont asking for three dollars.

I saw him last night.

This is what happened.

Delphine and I were walking to the Denny's door.

We saw 3 Dollars.

We knew instantly what was going to happen.

We got closer to the door.

3 Dollars said, "Did you see those cops down there, they got somebody."

For some reason 3 Dollars likes to have a conversation.

Then ask you for the three dollars.

I said back to 3 Dollars, "No, man. Where was it? Did you see it?" Delphine and I continued walking toward Denny's.

The whole time, 3 Dollars kept trying to bring the conversation back to him so he could ask us for three dollars.

He was like, "Yeah, I saw. But, wait. Hold on! I saw it. Hey, where you going?"

We went into Denny's and left him to ask someone else for three dollars.

THE LOOK

When I was about twelve.

I pissed off my father.

About what, who the fuck knows.

I was sitting in my bedroom and he came in and started saying shit to me.

Then he left.

I yelled, "You're fucking stupid!"

Which was true.

He didn't know much of anything, and had no interest in knowing about anything.

He was down the hall when I called him stupid.

He turned around.

Bolted at me.

Jumped on me.

Starting punching me in the face and chest.

Screaming obscenities at my head.

His face was full of anger.

Throbbing hatred.

Terror.

Horror.

I remember looking up at his face.

His anger had nothing to do with me.

I set something off in him.

Some pain.

Some terror of the past.

A truth he could not stand to take.

I was beaten brutally by my father several times, and I don't think I ever did anything that bad.

His anger was at the world.

At other people.

At his employers.

They had stolen his life.

His time.

His work.

All stolen.

I didn't know what his anger was derived from when I was twelve, but in my twenty-forth year of human existence I'm starting to learn.

A FLY ON A STOMACH

At Willow Lake, a camp outside of Youngstown where supposedly the biggest cement pool in the world was (at least that is what the sign says.)

In the humid and shitty heat of Ohio, John and Tessa hung out for the night camping, drinking and smoking weed.

They were just friends.

Tessa wouldn't date John because she only dated guys who made her look cool.

John was a dork and couldn't perform that function for her.

Tessa was four eleven, skinny, and looked like a twelve-year-old.

John was six three, muscular. White trash.

Tessa got extremely drunk and stoned.

She told John, "I gotta go to sleep, I'm so tired John, so fucked up." Tessa left the fire and John and went inside the tent to sleep.

She unzipped her sleeping bag and got inside, zipped it back up, and immediately passed out.

John sat around the fire and thought, I wanna fuck Tessa so bad.

Why won't she fuck me.

I paid her way.

I bought the beer and the weed.

She fucking owes me.

I don't understand.

I'm sexy, aren't I?

I'm more attractive than her last boyfriend.

Why won't she fuck me?

John sat there for an hour thinking these thoughts while drinking American beer and taking hits off the bowl.

He eventually got up and went into the tent.

He lay beside her, thinking, "Why doesn't she fuck me, why doesn't she fuck me, why doesn't she fuck me, I love her so much, why doesn't she fuck me!"

Eventually his thoughts led to this: She won't fuck me, I'll fuck her. As soon as I put it in, she'll love me, she'll know that I love her. It'll be just like it is in the movies.

John slowly unzipped her sleeping bag.

Then he crawled in beside her.

Got on top of her.

Kissed her face.

He unbuttoned her pants and pushed them down.

The whole time, Tessa remained sleeping.

John pushed her pants and underwear all the way past her feet.

Took his hard dick out.

Tessa woke up.

Looked at John and said not in terror but like she was speaking to a fly, "Get off of me you asshole, what the fuck do you think you're doing?"

John got scared and ran out of the tent.

John ran into the woods near the campsite.

He sat on the ground with his legs crossed, lit a joint, and cried.

Tessa thought in her head as she went back to sleep, That John, what a fucking loser.

*

My mother also said that all novels should have at least one rape. So there's one, Mom. Do you like it?

THE OLD MEN

Joe and I were sitting around at my house drinking BV and Coke, bullshitting for no apparent reason.

Monco: "So, how's your dad?"

Joe: "He's a crazy fucking asshole."

Monco: "Where's he working nowadays?"

Joe: "He sweeps the floor at a hardware store."

Monco: "From having a good job at a distribution center to sweeping floors, that's a damn shame."

Joe: "Ain't that the truth. How's your dad?"

Monco: "Haven't seen the asshole for a while, but I assume he's still working at K-mart."

Joe: "Goes from working at the family store, working with his family and friends, to working at the corporate shithole that put him out of work."

Monco: "Yup."

Joe: "That's a damn shame."

Monco: "Ain't that the truth."

Joe: "Is John's dad's work still locked-out?"

Monco: "No, I saw on the news the other day, that place is done. They've been locked-out so long they gotta close."

Joe: "Well fuck me, Jesus."

Monco: "You hear about Jack's dad. I hear he collects the money from pop machines now."

Joe: "That's what I heard too. The man goes from being three years away from his retirement at the steel mill to collecting quarters."

Monco: "Fuck me Jesus."

Joe: "Yes, fuck me Jesus."

APHORISMS

1. People who say "these" or "those" people are always "these" or "those" people.

2. If you feel like you are in a movie but aren't even the star and sometimes not even an extra, it is because the people around you are play-acting and you aren't.

3. If you feel alienated, you're right.

4. Before mowing the lawn, check and see if you have enough gas. It looks funny half-finished.

5. If you are having sex with someone and they start crying and you know it doesn't have anything to do with you, leave!

6. People who say that Republican-Christians have warped what the Bible conveys have not read the Bible. They follow it perfectly.

7. Religion is campy.

8. If you are hungry and have little money, eat three slices of bread. Wait twenty minutes and you feel like you are full.

9. There is no reason to care what other people think about you. Because seeing how this world is, it is obvious humans are not good thinkers.

10. If you don't have health insurance, are in insane debt, have warrants out on you, a mullet, several children, a shitty car, and a girlfriend missing three teeth, you can remain alive. You will not die from those things.

11. There is a statute of limitations on all types of bills, if you don't have the money. Go online and see how long you have to wait. But whatever you do, don't say you will pay the bill because the statute of limitations starts over then.

12. Your parents do not own you.

13. The government does not own you.

14. You do not own your lover and they do not own you.

15. If you decide you are going to kill someone, make sure it is a person you really want to kill.

16. Crackheads have their reasons.

17. If you have sex with one of your relatives it is not the end of the world.

18. All poor people are thieves. So are rich people. Some are just better at hiding it than others.

19. Charity is a confession of guilt.

20. People do change, but not always for the better.

21. Be wary of people who do not change.

22. When meeting people it is more important to judge not their intelligence but their level of fear.

23. Everyone thinks their baby is a genius.

24. There are only three things that link humans together: labor, sex, and terror.

25. The souls of the poor are hatred and violence.

27. What people love about God is not that he controls the world or built it, but that his ownership cannot be destroyed. Nobody can buy or steal what he owns. God also never dies.

28. Love is behavior.

29. If someone says, "I didn't have a dime to my name," they are lying; they know one of their rich relatives will eventually help them.

30. Question: Why don't the American poor admit that they are poor? Answer: If they admitted it, they would gain a world and that terrifies them.

31. A very irresponsible person will suddenly become very responsible when it comes to free money.

32. Sluts are people who know how to have a good time.

33. The core American value is sadism.

34. People who say, "That's a bad neighborhood," have reduced the residents of that neighborhood to mythological animals and themselves into gods.

35. There are no good people.

36. There are no good parents.

37. If a person says, "He or she has a good heart," it is guaranteed that that person is an asshole.

38. If a person is bipolar, it implies that they are an asshole.

39. There is a big difference between the phrases, "He says what he feels," and, "He tells it like it is." Michael Savage "says what he feels." Charles Bukowski "tells it like it is." Do you see the difference?

40. People never make four good choices in a row. If you can do three consistently, you're pretty damn good.

DRIVING DELPHINE TO WORK

When I drive Delphine to work at the bikini bar.
Her panties are still wet from washing them in the tub.
On the way to work we listen to classic rock.
And she dries her panties on the heater in the car.

THE RUST BELT

I'm alive.
So what?
My head hurts!
Take more pills.
I got gas.
Take more pills.
My hemorrhoids have swelled and I can't shit.
Jam Preparation H up my asshole.
I can't get to sleep because I can't stop thinking.
Drink more booze.
Joe's dad at the distribution center had TVs fall thirty feet onto his back.
Now he can barely move.
I hear from Joe he sits up all night smoking in the dark.
Lighting the next cigarette with the cigarette he just got done with.
My mother's back is destroyed too.
She hooks up electric things to her back.

She doesn't have any teeth either.

My grandmother got shock treatments and remains on heavy tranquilizers.

Joe used to be on Paxil for his anxiety.

He says he gets worried a lot.

He drinks a lot, I don't blame him.

My father takes vitamins so he can outlive my mom.

Sitcoms don't have drug addicts on them.

If they do it is for only one episode and the problem is solved by the end of it.

Sitcoms don't have husbands who beat their wives.

They don't have useless no-good mothers.

They don't swear, don't belittle each other.

The fights on sitcoms are so contrived and considerate.

Married people fight when one or both of them is drunk.

Parents on sitcoms don't smoke weed.

My dad smokes weed.

A lot of parents do.

My parents never behaved like the people on sitcoms, but they tried to in certain situations, in language and never behavior.

I was confused a lot as a child.

My parents always said I would grow up to work.

Have health insurance and children.

But work doesn't bring happiness.

Just broken backs.

Anger.

The need for drugs.

Booze.

And arguments.

My father broke lamps, phones, plates, and TVs when he got angry.

DO YOU

Do you think this really matters?

I mean it.

Do you?

Do you want money for this?

What would I do with it?

Buy a pool and overdose on cocaine in it.

Maybe get a tattoo or a cornflower blue jumpsuit.

Or some rims or a signed Dale Earnhardt shirt.

What about fame, would you take that?

Yeah, that would be awesome; everyone would know my name and what my face looked like.

Is that all fame is, people knowing your name and what your face looks like?

Well, yeah, but that's awesome.

What about happiness?

Oh, I gave up on that a long time ago. I once got the money to go on a two week vacation and it almost killed me. My brain isn't used to long-term happiness.

What about love? You want love, don't you? You deserve that, right?

Oh, fuck man, to love someone just means to me the person you go out with is the person you hate least in the world.

What if God came down from heaven and apologized to you?

I don't think I would care; none of this was His fault.

What if all the Presidents of the United States of America apologized to you personally for this?

I would tell them to go fuck themselves.

Do you know what has been done to you?

No, but I'm sure it's bad.

It is.

KARAOKE

I went to karaoke the other day.

It was a cold and ugly night.

Karaoke takes place on a Wednesday at a bar that has underground bands play there on the weekends.

Lately no bands play there.

I assume because the gas prices and the depression have hit Youngstown hard and people can't afford to go to schools, or even care about what bands come.

Karaoke is the only busy day the bar has anymore.

The people who go to karaoke aren't the same crowd that goes to the underground shows. It consists of college kids, punks, has-been preppies, white trash, and the locals in the neighborhood.

You can tell when it is a local because the person will be missing some teeth, dressed in Wal-Mart clothes, and half the time on crack.

I sat down at the bar and ordered a BV and Coke.

The bartender brought it over; he's this tall guy, yells a lot, funny, and a damn good bartender.

I looked around while I was there.

Noticed a lot of people were wearing costumes.

There were females wearing pointy-toed shoes, jeans with thrift-store skirts on top, strange blouses I don't how to describe, and Pat Benatar hair.

There were guys wearing suits, completely decked out in punk outfits even though they were rich kids, and a lot of kids had scarves on even though they were inside a building.

Nobody really talks to me at that bar.

I've pissed a lot of people off there.

For three different reasons: sex, vomit, and politics.

I've had sex with at least five different people who were in the bar that night.

Got in a physical altercation with a Republican.

And vomited on some kid's drum set.

I told him I had food poisoning.

That was bullshit, although I felt he deserved it.

I didn't even know why I was there. It was lame.

I decided to walk to the back room where karaoke takes place to see if there were any fine pieces of ass back there.

I walked back there carrying my BV and Coke.

I stood in front of the stage.

Some has-been preppy was singing an Elton John song. I think it was "Tiny Dancer."

I like "Tiny Dancer" so I listened.

The guy was singing his heart out up there.

He was a good singer too.

He hit the notes and didn't fuck up at all.

I started to sing along with it.

A lot of people were.

There were like eight people by the stage singing and dancing a little.

As I stared at him, I realized why there are karaoke and open mic nights.

It's because during school people are given all these chances to play sports, sing, act in plays, be in the band, all kinds of shit. But when they graduate it's all over, so many chances are taken away when a person graduates. A lot of fun is just cut off.

I started to cry a little when the guy started singing the chorus.

I knew at that moment there wasn't much difference between that has-been preppy's singing and my writing.

He just wanted to take a break from the shit of the world and express himself, have fun, and share his talents with other people, even if only eight other people cared.

SLEEPING FEMALE

I knew this girl in high school.

Don't remember her name; it isn't important.

On the weekends she used to take sleeping pills.

She would get home from school and take two sleeping pills.

Sleep till four in the morning.

She would walk to the kitchen.

Light a cigarette.

Get a glass of orange juice.

Take three sleeping pills.

Then she would go upstairs to her room.

Lie in bed smoking.

Staring into space.

Then close her eyes and fall asleep.

She would wake up around noon Saturday.

Walk to the kitchen.

Get a glass of orange juice.

Take four sleeping pills.

Go back to her room.

Lie in bed.

Smoke cigarettes.

Stare into space.

Then close her eyes and fall asleep.

Around nine o'clock Saturday night she would wake up again.

Go to the kitchen.

Get ham and cheese out of the refrigerator.

Make a ham sandwich.

Get some orange juice.
Take four sleeping pills.
Go to her bedroom.
Eat the ham sandwiches.
And fall asleep.
Around six Sunday morning she would wake up.
Go to the kitchen.
Get a cup of orange juice.
Take five sleeping pills.
Go to her bedroom.
And smoke cigarettes till she went to sleep.
Sunday afternoon, she woke up again.
Would go to the kitchen.
Her family was eating then.
There was pot roast on the kitchen table.
Nobody spoke to each other.
She would sit down and eat a few scraps of meat.
Then she would take six sleeping pills.
Go back to bed.
And smoke cigarettes till she fell asleep.
At four Monday morning she woke up.
Instead of going downstairs.
She would lie in her bed and smoke.
And go to school when the time came.

FAMILY

In a small living room with nice furniture and a color TV bought by the mother's dad.

Sat a Youngstown family eating dinner.

The mother sat on the couch drinking a forty.

The father on the floor.

Three children sitting about the room.

The dad got up and walked to the kitchen, bumping the mother's leg with his leg on the way there.

The mother said, "Hey motherfucker, you did that on purpose!"

The kids didn't look up.

"I didn't fucking do it on purpose," said the father.

"I know you fucking did, don't bullshit me. I know you, you're starting shit!"

"Whatever."

He went to the kitchen.

Came back to the living room.

Sat on the floor and continued to eat dinner.

The mother stared in anger while she ate.

She sat there for about ten minutes pretending calmly to watch the television.

She stood up.

Kicked the father in the back of head.

His head flew forward.

She slammed her plate on his head.

Then sprinted for the door.

Flung her forty of beer at him and ran outside.

The mother stayed outside for about ten minutes letting the father cool off.

Then she came back in and sat on the couch like nothing happened.

The father was sitting on the couch and said to her, "I should so kick your ass, but I know you'll call the fucking police and I don't need that shit."

The kids never looked up the whole time.

DENNY'S

I like to go to Denny's.

It is nice there.

The servers are nice.

The service isn't bad, and most of the customers aren't assholes.

I was sitting there for a few hours one day.

Relaxing, being pointless, doing nothing.

The Arabs were there, they are always there between the hours ten and one at night, and then they leave.

I think they're Saudis and they own gas stations.

Not sure though.

Arabs own all the non-corporate mini-marts and gas stations.

I have no idea why; maybe there was a movement in the Middle East to infiltrate America through mini-marts and gas stations.

Probably not. That sounds really stupid.

Hell, I don't know, and I don't really care.

But they sit at Denny's every night and if you talk to them, they are friendly.

The server that night was Chuck. He has an extreme lisp and doesn't give a fuck about his job.

He doesn't care to the point that when you want some more to drink, you have to get up and find him half the time.

I don't care. Getting up and finding him gives me something to do.

And he's a lot better than Gina, who talks your ear off about her husband, I don't know his name. She only refers to him as "my husband." Which is common among Youngstown women.

Gina is like twenty-two and her husband is like eighteen. I don't know how that happened.

She probably had a dad who was a rolling stone, as people like to say, and now she wants a little boy to control. Which happens a lot in Youngstown.

I've never seen anyone in Youngstown get married for good reasons.

As psychologists and most anybody knows, people stay in relationships because they share the same value structure.

Most of the values I see that keep people "in love" are:

- drug addiction.
- mediocrity.
- inertness of thought.
- racism.
- laziness.
- lameness.
- self-loathing.
- violence.
- alcoholism.
- to control someone and be controlled by someone else.
- love of objects.
- pretending they are richer than they are.
- money.

Yeah, that's marriage in Youngstown.

That's Youngstown love, baby.

My parents' values are in that group.

While I was at Denny's I drank a hot tea.

I can't drink coffee.

It makes me vomit.

I used to drink tons of it, you know, I would sit with my Kerouac book, drink coffee, and be cool.

For some reason I started vomiting every time I drank coffee.

So I don't drink it anymore.

Now I drink hot tea.

No honey or lemons.

The hot water with a tea bag and two Sweet N'Low sugars.

People tell me all the time that Sweet N'Low gives people cancer, I don't know about that and don't really care.

I think the only reason I use Sweet N'Low instead of regular sugar is because back in the day when I started drinking coffee I wasn't paying attention and just put the Sweet N'Low in and just got used to it over time, and now regular sugar doesn't taste right.

I was reading a Steve Kostecke zine.

It was really good and fun to read.

While I was reading the Kostecke zine, a group of white trash people came in.

Two dirty-looking dudes with goatees, an overweight girl with bad skin, and this strange-looking chubby faced girl with HUGE blonde hair.

I wanted to fuck her; you could tell that without the HUGE blonde hair she was plain and almost ugly.

But with the huge blonde hair she looked hot.

It kind of didn't look right on her.

She must have seen the hair on a rich girl in a magazine.

Denny's has several customers that are there every night.

One person is this black old guy who wears a shitty green trench coat, a black hoodie, and he looks like hell on a stick.

He rarely ever speaks, and is always polite.

I once found him sleeping in the bathroom.

Another is this old German immigrant who doesn't wash or comb his hair.

He wears blue jogging pants, never talks to anyone, and looks like he could kill you without thinking twice about it.

And he looks like hell on a stick.

One person is this young Arab kid; he looks like a dork, rarely ever speaks, and always looks like he is going to cry.

There is one more regular; I almost forgot about him because he sits in the non-smoking section.

He's an older black man who wears thrift store clothing and carries a black leather bag with him.

He always sits in non-smoking.
Orders two cokes and a milkshake.
He usually takes something out of his bag and reads.
He also looks like hell on a stick.

I finished the Kostecke zine and left. There was nothing else to do there. And to stare into space at Denny's is just demoralizing.

NOTE: This story was written in 2005. Since then, Steve Kostecke has died. RIP.

FIRST MEMORY

I was about four years old.
Tiny Monco.
I was alone in the bathtub.
My parents never helped me take a bath.
They didn't care if I washed my hair or wiped my ass.
To this day, I've never gotten used to washing my hair.
I was lying in the bathtub playing around.
Poking at my pecker and licking the soap.
Then I started to hear these horrible noises coming from the living room.
It sounded like my dad was beating up my mom.
I got very scared.
I sat in the bathtub paralyzed.
Eventually I got the balls to get up and see if Daddy was killing Mommy.
I stepped out of the bathtub naked and crept to the living room.
My daddy was on top of my mommy's back while she lay on the floor. He pumped her butt wildly.
Both of their pants were down.
My mother was screaming loudly.
I was horrified.
I ran back to the tub, got in, and stayed there.
Eventually, the screaming ended.
It looked like my father brutally beat my mother.
I was four and had no idea what sex was; I had no idea what they were doing.
I sat in the bathtub, hoping one of them would come in and tell me what I saw.

But they never did.

The weirdest thing of all is that my favorite sexual position is to have the girl lie on her stomach and for me to lie on top of her back and hump her butt.

THE STATE-FUNDED DENTIST

Getting my cavities filled at the state-funded dentist's office went like this.

They called me in from the waiting room.

I went to the back. It was a big space with six open rooms. There were three dentists and four nurses there.

All the dentists and nurses were very young.

There was a five-year-old black kid screaming bloody murder in one of the little open rooms.

His mom was telling him to shut the fuck up and to take it like a man.

I sat down in one of the little rooms. One of the young dentists came over and sat by me. They have yet to tell me her name and she's worked on my teeth four times. The nurse was a young female who went to one of the fifty local vocation schools that teach nursing.

The dentist never spoke to me.

Never asked my name.

What I do for a living.

How big my dick is.

Nothing.

Which I liked.

My last dentist wouldn't stop asking me stupid questions about college, girlfriends, my brothers, all kinds of stupid shit.

The dentist didn't give a fuck about me.

She began shooting Novocain into my mouth.

She shot a total of four to five shots.

That shocked me because my last dentist did no more than two. But I soon figured out why.

The dentist got her grinding tools and started pulverizing my teeth.

The teeth she was working on looked like hell.

They were brown.

Had parts chipped off.

You could see the cavities from fifteen feet away.

While she was grinding my teeth away.

The dentist and the nurse had a conversation about their uterine cancers.

The dentist had cancer last year but it was cured and the nurse was soon going to get a biopsy because she was suspected of having cancer.

The nurse had two kids and a husband and she was worried about that.

The dentist had a dog.

Usually in dentists' offices, after every two minutes or so, the nurse gives you a cup of cold water to put in your mouth, swirl around, and spit out.

They didn't do that.

The nurse just held a spit vacuum in my mouth, that's all.

At times I was choking on blood.

But then the nurse would just let me hold the spit vacuum to get the blood out.

The way the dentist worked on my teeth was very different than my old dentist.

My old dentist, the one my mother's health insurance kind of paid for, would do one tooth at a time and then move on to the next one.

The state-funded dentist ground all three teeth up.

Threw the filling on top of all three of them.

Then did the laser pointer thing with all three.

It was as if she was making three ham sandwiches.

Very assembly line-like.

It went quickly though.

Soon my teeth looked good as new.

I was very happy about that.

Out of all the things that have come out, advances in technology, computers, cell phones, cars, etc. I would say if someone asked me, "If you could save one piece of technology from destruction, what would it be?" I would answer the technological advances in dentistry.

SOMETHING WAS MISSING

I was at a giant supermarket the other night.

It was three in the morning.

Delphine was with me getting food.

When we were waiting in line to check out.

I noticed the guy in line in front of us had something over his nose.

It was a plastic shield.
I realized why it was there.
He had no nose!
The man had no nose!
The man's nose was gone!
It was fucking horrifying!

A GREAT MENACE WEIGHS OVER THE CITY

Back in '96.

A fourteen-year-old girl and her little sister were walking down the street.

It was a sunny day.

Some clouds. But the pretty white ones.

The girls lived in a cramped apartment with a mother who was drunk all the time.

A stepfather who was drunk all the time and liked to take the phone apart to look at the wires.

A van pulled to the side of the road.

A man jumped out.

The girls stood confused for a second.

Then the man pulled his dick out and started jacking off.

The girls screamed and ran.

The man got back in his van and drove home.

He got home.

His wife was there.

He went to the living room and sat down in his favorite seat.

His wife came in and screamed at him, "You no-good piece of shit!

"You are so fucking stupid!

"Can't you do anything!

"What's fucking wrong with you!

"Go mow the lawn you lazy no-good fucking piece of shit!"

American Sketches

THE DISH TANK

When I was nineteen I lived and worked at the Grand Canyon.

I worked there for a month until they fired me for drinking.

I worked at El Tovar.

The most expensive restaurant at the Grand Canyon.

Presidents, rock stars, if you had money you ate at El Tovar when you went to the Grand Canyon.

One table of six could amass a six hundred dollar bill at dinner.

I worked in the dish tank.

The reason I worked in the dish tank was because I was American and not in a good college.

The Grand Canyon got workers from all over the world through some program I can't remember the name of.

If you were from Russia, France, Iceland, etcetera they would put you in the front of the house as a busboy or server.

It also worked the same way with kids from good colleges like Yale and Harvard.

The reason they would have the foreign workers work in the front of the house was because the name tags at the Grand Canyon specified where you were from. And the rich tourists would look at the people's name tags and see Holland or England and think it was great.

They also only had to work three to four days a week for no more than four hours at a time while dishwashers worked five to six days a week ten hours at a time.

The front of the house people made more money per hour than the dishwashers.

They made $5.35 plus tips. We made $5.35 with no tips.

The people who had to do dishes were Americans from states like Illinois and Ohio, and the Native Americans.

There were two dish areas.

A front area where plates, cups, and silverware were cleaned.

And a back area where pots and kitchen utensils were cleaned.

The room where the kitchen shit was cleaned was a hellhole.

The walls had all the paint crusted off.

The garbage was filled with dead fish.

Old soup.

Meat.

It smelled like hell in there.

The room was filled with steam from the hot water.

There was a metal stand to put the dirty pots on.

There was a small radio that played the Grand Canyon radio station which was just the same four bad songs over and over again.

There were three huge sinks.

One to soak the plates.

One to wash them.

One to sanitize them.

Two guys worked that room together.

For the month I worked there, I worked with about seven different people because the Grand Canyon fired people constantly.

When I first got there, the head of the dish tank was this deranged old wastoid named Chuck.

He was about fifty years old.

Had a handlebar mustache.

Had worked at over five national parks.

He once said this to me: "I remember one of my past lives. I was a slave master in the Old South. I remember being in charge of a huge plantation."

I looked at him and said nothing.

He would talk like everything he said would be life-altering and earth-shattering, which is common among people who don't know shit about anything.

The guy wasn't miserable though.

He loved living in beautiful places and having new experiences.

Which isn't bad.

I knew a lot of people way more intelligent than him back in Youngstown, but they never had the balls to be happy.

Even though Chuck was dumb as shit, he always found a way to live in beautiful places.

Then after a shitty day of work he could walk to the edge of the Grand Canyon or to the hot springs of Yellowstone and smile.

The second in command was José, a Hopi Indian.

He had the most horrible teeth I have ever seen on a human being.

They were all black and broken up.

They looked like black gravel in his mouth.

It was fucking horrible when he smiled.

José would work really hard and look miserable the whole time.

He didn't talk much either and no one could understand what he said.

He had a really thick Hopi accent.

The weird thing about José was that he could disappear and reappear out of nowhere.

Like you would turn around and José would be gone or you would look back and José was standing there.

You would say, "José, how long you been there? You scared the fuck out of me." And he would respond, "Like ten minutes." It was fucking weird.

José was a drunk.

As were most of the Indians at the Grand Canyon.

Well hell, most of the Americans working at the Grand Canyon were drunks too.

José didn't show up to work one day because he decided to not stop drinking while down in Flagstaff and they fired him.

Which was sad because he was a really good dishwasher.

I saw him before he left the Grand Canyon and he said that he was going to another park deeper into Arizona to work.

One American who worked there was a nineteen-year-old named Dave.

He was this complete jerk-off from Illinois.

He would constantly talk about OSHA and how we couldn't do certain shit because it was unsanitary.

The other dishwashers would stare at him like an asshole and tell him he was stupid.

There isn't much that can be said about him except that he was a big loser.

There were some other dishwashers but they were either there at the beginning of when I got there and or at the end when I got fired.

SELLING MOVIES

One night at the Grand Canyon.

I was up all night drinking with some kid from New Zealand.

His name was Tom, a nice kid.

He had grown up in New Zealand, had an American mother and a Kiwi father.

I guess his family had money back in New Zealand and he was just passing through.

He was kind of a backpacker but backpackers never go near real people and stay on their scheduled route and only speak to other backpackers.

Tom was different, but he didn't care.

There was a sense of hopelessness and disillusion about him that I think brought him to enjoy the company of lower class people like myself and the other dishwashers at the Grand Canyon.

Whatever made him feel like that, I don't know.

Well, one night we had stayed up the whole night in the community TV room of the dorm talking about our lives and other people's lives, and whatever thoughts came to our drunken brains.

The sun eventually came up and we were sitting there about ready to go to sleep and then this old beat-to-shit Indian came in, sat next to us, pulled out *Top Gun* from his pocket, showed it to us and said, "You wanna buy this video?"

Tom and I stared at him, wondering what the hell was happening.

We both said, "No thank you."

Then the Indian put the video back in his pocket and left.

Tom was like, "What was that?"

"I don't know," I said.

THE FEATHER

It was the Fourth of July at the Grand Canyon.

No fireworks because of the dryness of Arizona.

A lot of drinking though.

I was sitting in the community TV room with like six other guys.

There was Martinez Whitehair, an Indian who was completely insane.

That day he wore socks up to his knees, shorts, and a plain white t-shirt.

When he was drunk he would go on for hours about how the Navajo language came from the rabbits, how people need to respect the dishes they wash, how the Grand Canyon was created by Noah's ark, and how the Elders are racist.

There was a fat guy named Bob who had a handlebar mustache, was bald, and fucking stupid.

He would never get drunk.

But would talk about how people can lift themselves up by their bootstraps all night.

I would argue with the fucker all night.

I didn't have a clue what I was talking about.

But random people would say they thought I was right.

There was a guy named Michael who was African-American and very pissed all the time.

He was one of the most intelligent people I've ever met.

He made me look stupid constantly. Everything I told him, he would tell me I was wrong.

As the years passed I would find he was right, and not because I was looking for the answers he gave me.

But because after I figured it out I would think, "Holy shit, Michael told me that at the Grand Canyon two years ago!"

I wish I could find Michael to tell him what I learned and to learn more from him but he's gone.

They are all gone and if there are any left they will be gone one day too.

Tom was also there.

We were all sitting there having a nice Fourth of July talk and then a middle-aged broken-looking Indian comes in and sits down on one of the couches, drinking a tall boy and carrying three more with him.

He had on a ball cap with one feather in it.

Bob the fat guy asked the Indian how he got the feather.

The Indian looked at us and said, "In Vietnam."

The darkness is coming, I thought.

The Indian with the feather began his monologue on the Fourth of July.

The monologue was scatterbrained.

The man obviously had been drinking heavily for over thirty years and had what is called Mush Brain. Which is common among older people who have spent their lives drinking and doing drugs and have been through too many absurd and terrifying experiences.

It is when a normal person can barely communicate with the outside any longer. They have an inability to form paragraphs and sentences to convey complete thoughts. You can tell when speaking to them that they know what they are talking about and they know what you're talking about. But they have killed too many brain cells and just can't do it anymore.

The Indian with the feather basically told us.

He went to Vietnam on the Fourth of July back in '68.

That he thought it was bullshit that he had to go because the Vietnamese weren't doing shit to him but he was drafted and didn't want to go to prison.

He was there on the front lines because he said if you were a minority that is where you immediately went.

He snuck away from the American side and found a small village and found some Vietnamese people to live with.

Waited till after the war was done to go back to America.

While speaking he kept telling us he saw babies burned alive.

"I saw babies burned alive!

"I saw babies burned alive!

"I saw babies burned alive!

"I saw babies burned alive!"

How he saw useless death all the time.

Everyone in the room barely said anything during his monologue.

There was no need to interrupt him.

We wanted to hear what he had to say and we didn't want him to get off track.

He didn't say it like it would change our lives either.

He said it like it had changed his life.

He didn't really care who he told or who was listening.

He just knew it had to be said.

I would not doubt that he told that monologue to a different group of people every Fourth of July and that he will tell it till he dies.

THE YOKE

After I got fired from the Grand Canyon I moved to San Diego.

It was one of the biggest culture shocks of my life.

The first week there I'm sure I just walked around and stared at everything like I'd entered an alternate reality.

Everything in San Diego in 2000 after the great bull market of the nineties looked shiny, glossy, and new.

The streets were perfectly paved and clean.

Not a cigarette butt to be found on a sidewalk.

All the buildings were less than ten years old and if they were older they were remodeled to look like new.

When you walked down the street, people didn't give you the "I'll cut your fucking balls off" look that is common in Youngstown.

Youngstown was a third world country compared to the neon newness of San Diego.

When we first got to San Diego, we sometimes went to the beach and sat on the wall separating the beach from the boardwalk.

Watched people ride by on bikes or just jogging.

We would sit there for hours, staring at the people going by, talking shit about them as they passed.

Most of them except the Mexicans seemed very concerned with how they looked.

They wanted pretty faces, strong muscles, and basically to look cool and sexy.

Tom and I looked homeless, which we were. We'd been sleeping in gas station parking lots in my '89 Caprice Classic.

There were a lot of homeless people at the beach.

Most of them were your stereotypical homeless.

Shaggy beards.

Ripped t-shirts.

Dirty hair.

Most of them delivered papers and did construction under the table for forty dollars a day.

Some would wonder why they didn't save up and buy nice clothes to get a job.

The truth is, forty dollars a day didn't buy shit in San Diego in 2000 and probably buys even less now.

The money went to eating a cheeseburger at Jack in the Box and the rest went to booze.

I remember one homeless man who collected cans on the beach.

When you were on a San Diego beach, you would just throw your beer and soda cans on the beach so the homeless wouldn't have to sift through the garbage to get them.

I remember an old, almost dead Chinese man who was wearing the traditional blue Mao Communist outfit.

He had built a yoke out of a plastic pipe and attached two huge garbage bags to the ends.

He carried it down the beach with no emotion at all.

I doubt he had time for emotions.

He would put his yoke down and pick up some cans and put them into one of the bags.

Then pick up the yoke again and walk down the beach.
I sat and watched that.
It was real and could not be denied.

CHINESE FOOD AND URINATION

I was in downtown San Diego one day in 2000.
I was hungry and looking for cheap food.
I stumbled upon this Chinese food cafeteria that served a Styrofoam bowl of one food item for ninety-nine cents.
I went in.
It looked like it had booths from a closed down fast-food restaurant.
It was bare.
Not even one of those pictures of Hong Kong on the wall.
Walked up to the counter and picked out three items for three dollars.
Then sat down and ate.
There were a lot of homeless there.
There were perhaps more homeless in downtown San Diego than on the beaches.
The homeless all had cuts and bruises.
Most of them were crazy or had chosen, through the sick and brutal contingency of experience, that it was better to be drunk, on crack, to drop out.
That to face the rigid routine and institutions of work, family, romance, and upholding false notions was too much for them to bear.
That to be drunk or on drugs, and without those institutions, existence was better and easier to face.
I always gave the homeless a dollar or two and bought them cheese-burgers.
I didn't give them money and food because I thought it was my duty or some form of charity.
But because I understood. I had traveled two-thousand five-hundred miles to San Diego to escape my life.
I knew what drove people to escape, the causes that make it very possible for a person to just say, "Go fuck yourself, world. What good have you done for me anyway!"
It wasn't charity.
It was solidarity.

A oneness in the understanding that the shit of life never ends, and that we are all victims of a mass hysteria of stupidity.

I left the cafeteria and walked down the street. While walking I saw a homeless woman covertly pull down her pants and piss on one of the big bank buildings.

I laughed and walked on.

WE THE PEOPLE

While I lived in San Diego, I stayed in a small boarding house.

I lived in a decent-sized room with Tom, the kid from New Zealand.

The room had two single beds, a closet and a sink with a small mirror, and a television with cable.

We had to share a kitchen and a bathroom with the other renters.

Through this sharing I met the other people who lived there.

The person who ran the boarding house was named Alex.

He was an ex-marine who fought in Vietnam and got shot.

Then he was a cop and got shot there too.

Then for someone reason got involved in doing drugs and got shot twice while doing that.

He loved to show people his bullet wounds.

He was very proud of them.

Alex also had an obsession with weapons. The office he worked in had ninja swords, guns, bows, and knives all over the walls.

He would show Tom and I his real expensive guns and swords all the time.

He was also obsessed with buying shit off of eBay like gold rings, necklaces, and tons of golden shit. That is also where he got his guns.

He would buy really expensive shit every day, which didn't make sense to Tom and I because he lived so cheaply and was so white trash.

We asked him about it one day and he said that back in the mid-nineties, he threw a bunch of money in Microsoft stock and made a shitload and immediately pulled it out.

Alex would sit all night in his room and watch porn.

And I mean all night.

The boarding house didn't have air-conditioning, so the windows would stay open all night.

Alex's window was on the first floor.

Every time Tom and I walked by his window at night, we could see porn on his television through the window.

There was a guy who everybody called the Chaplain.

Everybody called him the Chaplain because he claimed that he was a chaplain in the Navy for twenty years.

No one believed him though. He was completely insane.

The Chaplain had no job. Like most people in the boarding house, he got money from the government for being nuts.

The Chaplain would always start talking about God to you while you were cooking in the kitchen, not Christian Republican God talk, but his own cracked version of it. It would usually go like this: "See, God is like a flower.

"Delicate and beautiful.

"God, you know, made the universe from rocks and dust from an alien spaceship.

"Sometimes when I touch myself I feel that God wants me to.

"God doesn't want me to go to the mall.

"He knows how drunk I get when I become the Godhead and swim the thousand oceans of the devil and slithering snakes of shit and gargoyle breath.

"My brother once jammed a stick in my anus and God told me He did that to test me.

"God sent birds to attack my mother.

"God is going to return and take me to heaven to sit beside Him on the throne."

The Chaplain was insane.

At night he would sit at a desk till five in the morning, working.

Tom and I assumed it was on some strange long manuscript that resembled the word salad schizophrenic shit he would tell us while we were in the kitchen.

It gets weirder than that.

The whole time he worked at night, he wore a t-shirt pushed back on his head, kind of like a nun's habit.

The Chaplain was a madman.

With no apparent purpose but to do nothing and annoy people.

He was completely nuts and no one wanted him around.

There was an Islamic black girl named Fatima.

She wore soft dresses that covered her arms and legs.

She also wore a hijab that covered her hair.

She was attractive and very strange.

Fatima was married to some guy Tom and I never saw.

Fatima said that her husband had another wife and that he spent most of his time with her.

His other wife had the kids and took care of the nice house.

You got the impression she was his hot young wife that he supported and fucked for fun.

Fatima had no real problem with that.

Her husband paid her bills and gave her spending money.

I assumed Fatima took that deal because she was so fucked up in the head she couldn't work anywhere without getting fired within two weeks.

So it was like SSI without having to fuck around with the government.

On top of the boarding house, there was a roof with a deck where you could sit and look at downtown San Diego.

Fatima used to sit up there with us a lot.

She would tell us about her life before she was a Muslim.

She used to date a guy from Colombia who was involved in the drug trade, her mother was a Baptist preacher, she never knew her father and she used to do coke.

She was homeless when she was fifteen years old.

Sometimes she would do her prayers in front of us.

She would wash her arms, feet, legs, hands, and then pray to Allah.

Tom and I would stare at her, wondering what the hell she was doing.

It was obvious that she became Islamic because the world had taken too many shits on her head and Islam gave her a perfect escape from that.

The Muslims consistently gave her money, a place to stay, food, and filled her mind full of campy fantasies about heaven and some antichrist character with one eye.

As far as Tom and I could see, it was all one giant act to escape reality.

She had no interest in heaven; her main interest was shelter, food, and escape from the misery of her life.

There were two more strange characters living in the boarding house.

One was a thirty-something black guy and the other was a forty-something woman.

I don't recall their names.

All I remember about them is that the woman would give Tom and I food that tasted like shit.

She would give us refried beans that were three days old and leftover fried chicken. It was all disgusting.

Well, this is what happened one time with them.

I was alone in the kitchen making some Ramen noodles.

I was standing there waiting for them to be done.

They came into the kitchen and faced me like they were going to talk to me.

I looked at them, waiting to hear what absurd shit they were going to say to me.

"We would like to know if you would have sex with both of us at the same time," said the woman.

I looked at them and thought of that famous Hunter S. Thompson quote: "When the going gets weird, the weird turn pro."

"I'll do it for five hundred dollars apiece," I said.

"We don't got five hundred dollars apiece," said the woman.

"That's my offer."

"Come on man, just some sex," said the black guy.

"You obviously don't have money. I'm gonna get my Ramen, go upstairs, and eat it."

I got my Ramen and walked past them.

The black guy looked heartbroken.

I was very flattered.

THE MARINE CORPS

After I got home from San Diego, I got some money and went to see a childhood friend graduate from the Marines.

I went with another friend who knew him.

His name was Carl.

A nice guy. Short, stocky, very friendly, very nervous.

We got to the base and went to the graduation ceremony.

We sat in the stands with all the proud parents in hot-and-humid-as-fuck South Carolina in August.

It was hot, muggy, and just fucking ugly there.

We sat in the stands for a long time.

Then about a thousand Marines started marching out.

They marched perfectly.

All in a straight line.

All taking synchronized steps.

It was fucking insane.

Then some man yelled and they all stopped perfectly at the same time.

Then the man yelled several more times.

They made several fancy movements and finally, all at the same time, lined up their bodies in perfect precision, facing us with their legs apart and hands on their sides.

Carl and I were terrified.

There were a thousand young men just like me and him standing there on the hot concrete.

The thing that terrified me the most was that the ceremony was at least an hour long.

For the whole hour the young men just like me and Carl were standing there without moving, for an hour.

No fidgeting.

No scratching of the crotch.

Nothing.

No movement.

They stood in the exact same position for one hour straight without moving.

They were like robots.

The only time they moved was when the drill instructor gave a command, and then they would all move like perfectly synchronized robots.

It was terrifying!

That night my childhood friend who I grew up with.

Who enjoyed literature, music, and was very sensitive, told Carl and I about how the drill instructors would hit him, how fighting amongst each other if one didn't do their work right was encouraged.

How the drill instructors would make them guzzle water till they vomited.

That the drill instructors wouldn't let them piss, so they would piss themselves.

How every recruit, no matter how big they were, was driven to tears at least once.

How young men constantly tried to kill themselves.

But he said it like it was normal. You could see the terror in his face when describing boot camp, but there was no concrete realization of the horror of it.

Carl and I sat there terrified, listening to him speak of Marine boot camp.

The shit they demanded of them was humiliating and painful.

We both wondered why any human would put themselves into that situation and why they would not leave that situation if they made the mistake of getting into it.

My childhood friend came out of boot camp a completely new person.

First his body was turned into pure muscle, which he was very proud of.

He used to be proud of his paintings and the songs he made up, but now he was proud of his muscles.

His brain took a turn for the worse. He became very nervous, high strung, in a constant state of tension.

If things were not exact, he would freak out.

For example:

Carl and I drove him back to Ohio, and at a gas station I pumped like $22.64 of gas into the tank. I didn't mind not hitting an even number because I knew I was gonna buy some snacks and something to drink while I was in there.

But my childhood friend had a freak-out. "You're supposed to hit an even number when getting gas. Why didn't you just stop at twenty-two dollars?"

He looked at me and sounded like he wanted to punch my face in for that.

There were other little incidents but I don't remember them.

He was so used to sameness and everybody doing the same thing.

If someone didn't do something exactly the way he did, he freaked out.

Marine boot camp doesn't break a person down and rebuild them as a Marine.

No, it breaks them down and teaches them to keep themselves down.

It makes them terrified of those different from them, and makes them terrified to make their own choices.

Some of the most terrified and broken people I've ever met in my whole life are Marines.

They usually are separated into those two groups.

The broken.

The terrified.

There are the terrified ones who spend their whole lives placing everyone they meet into neat little categories.

Beating up people in bars and their family members and usually being racist and just a dick.

The broken Marines are different though.

They grew to hate the Marine Corps.

All the sameness and the turning of humans into objects pissed them off.

A lot entered combat and realized what humans are capable of doing to other humans.

A lot of them still call themselves Marines, but it is only to give some definition to their identity and to get the free breakfasts at the local veterans club.

I've met a good amount of broken ex-Marines and most of them are pleasant and fun to be around.

There are a good amount who are really broken though. My childhood friend is now a schizophrenic, cuts his own hair, is a drug addict, carries an umbrella around with him when there is no chance of rain, and has told people that he is the messiah, and he eats raw ground chuck because he thinks it is good for him.

THE BOWERY

In the winter of 2002, I took a trip to New York City.

I was in the Bowery.

It was five in the afternoon.

I was dressed in a cheap leather brown coat.

Had a hooded sweatshirt on with the sleeves popping out from the arms of the coat.

Unshaved.

Had on a cheap stocking cap and blue jeans.

And a pair of worn-out Reeboks.

I had two hundred dollars in my pocket.

I walked into a bar to get a drink.

You can drink all day in New York City because taxis will drive you everywhere.

I liked that about the city.

I had to piss so I went straight to the bathroom.

The bartender saw me and rushed from behind the bar.

He caught up with me and said, "You can't use the bathroom unless you are going to buy something."

I looked at him funny.

I was wearing what everybody in Youngstown wears and he thought I was homeless.

Then I became angry.

I said, "I'm gonna buy something. I have to piss."

Then the bartender gave me a rude look and went back behind the bar.

I clogged the sink with toilet paper and pissed in it.
Then went and sat at the bar.
The bartender came up to me.
I put a fifty on the bar and said, "Give me a Black Velvet and Coke."
"What's Black Velvet?" said the bartender.
"It's whiskey. You got Wild Turkey?"
"No, we don't have that either."
"You got Old Grandad?"
"No."
"Well, I guess I ain't drinking here."
I picked up my fifty and left.

ABOUT THE AUTHOR

Noah Cicero grew up in Youngstown, Ohio and later moved to South Korea. He is back in Ohio for now. His novel *GO TO WORK. DO YOUR JOB. CARE FOR YOUR CHILDREN. PAY YOUR BILLS. OBEY THE LAW. BUY PRODUCTS.* will be published by Lazy Fascist in August 2013.

ALSO FROM LAZY FASCIST

and many more!

www.ingramcontent.com/pod-product-compliance
Lightning Source LLC
Chambersburg PA
CBHW030128030726
47498CB00007B/2608